ABOUT

The author of more t[...] and adults, Janice Ka[...] Superromance novels [...] about the way generat[...] our earliest experiences have on us throughout life. Her 2007 novel *Snowbound* won a RITA® Award from Romance Writers of America for Best Contemporary Series Romance. A former librarian, Janice raised two daughters in a small rural town north of Seattle, Washington. She loves to read and is an active volunteer and board member for Purrfect Pals, a no-kill cat shelter.

Books by Janice Kay Johnson

HARLEQUIN SUPERROMANCE

1092—THE GIFT OF CHRISTMAS
"Undercover Santa"
1140—TAKING A CHANCE†
1153—THE PERFECT MOM†
1166—THE NEW MAN†
1197—MOMMY SAID GOODBYE
1228—REVELATIONS
1273—WITH CHILD
1332—OPEN SECRET*
1351—LOST CAUSE*
1383—KIDS BY CHRISTMAS*
1405—FIRST COMES BABY
1454—SNOWBOUND
1489—THE MAN BEHIND THE COP
1558—SOMEONE LIKE HER
1602—A MOTHER'S SECRET
1620—MATCH MADE IN COURT

†Under One Roof
*Lost...But Not Forgotten

HARLEQUIN EVERLASTING LOVE

21—CHRISTMAS PRESENTS AND PAST

SIGNATURE SELECT SAGA

DEAD WRONG

HARLEQUIN ANTHOLOGY

A MOTHER'S LOVE
"Daughter of the Bride"

HARLEQUIN SINGLE TITLE

WRONG TURN
"Missing Molly"

To my daughters, Sarah and Katie,
both smart, creative, caring young women
who make me proud every day.

Charlotte's Homecoming

Janice Kay Johnson

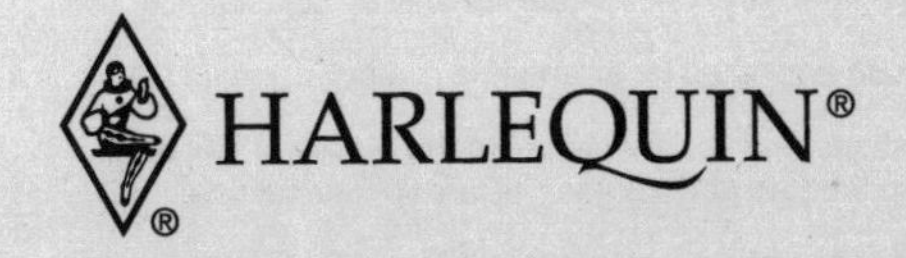

TORONTO • NEW YORK • LONDON
AMSTERDAM • PARIS • SYDNEY • HAMBURG
STOCKHOLM • ATHENS • TOKYO • MILAN • MADRID
PRAGUE • WARSAW • BUDAPEST • AUCKLAND

ISBN-13: 978-0-373-78389-2

CHARLOTTE'S HOMECOMING

This edition published by arrangement with Harlequin Books S.A.

For questions and comments about the quality of this book please contact us at Customer_eCare@Harlequin.ca.

www.eHarlequin.com

Printed in U.S.A.

"Charlotte, I'm going to have to kiss you."

Alarm kicked in at Gray's words, and she backed up, feeling the rustle of leaves. "What?"

His laugh was gone, his eyes intent on her face as one long step brought him close enough to crowd her. "You're gutsy about everything but me."

"Maybe I'm just not interested." She was dismayed to hear her voice emerge too high, betraying panic or desperation. "Did you ever think of that?"

"Hmm." His gaze dropped to her mouth. "Why don't we find out?"

She was dizzy, from the heat, from the thick air, from the frantic pace of her pulse. Would it be so terrible to find out what it felt like to be kissed by Gray?

Yes. She was terribly afraid that the answer was yes. But she'd never yet backed away from an accusation of cowardice, and she wouldn't do it now.

Be honest. You don't want to back away.

Dear Reader,

Here's one of those subjects fun to debate: are we the products of our childhood, or are we biologically driven to become who we are? Hmm. After raising two daughters of my own and countless litters of kittens (I'm an active volunteer with a no-kill cat shelter), I've come firmly down smack dab in the middle on the nature vs. nurture debate. Of course our childhoods influence us profoundly! And yet, there's simply no question that children—and kittens—are born already predisposed to be timid or adventurous, thoughtful or impetuous, ready to be happy or suspicious of every new face. Twins, now… Especially *identical* twins… Shouldn't they not only have the next best thing to an identical upraising while also being predisposed to have the same nature? But does it ever work like that?

Charlotte and Faith are not much alike at all. They share a powerful bond, and yet have spent years estranged because Faith desperately needs to be close while Charlotte, equally desperately, needs to know that she is unique. Only Charlotte's homecoming will save Faith's life…and free Charlotte to love.

Just like the lives of any twins, their stories are entangled and neither could be told entirely alone. So look for Faith's book, *Through the Sheriff's Eyes,* next month. Having two whole books to explore the characters and the men they love was great fun, too!

Happy reading,

Janice Kay Johnson

CHAPTER ONE

FAITH WAS WAITING IN THE gas station parking lot when the Airporter pulled in. Charlotte saw her right away, leaning against her Blazer, almost as battered as Dad's pickup, and for the same reason—it was a working vehicle. The fact that Faith—slender, graceful and feminine—would drive something like that suggested to Charlotte that she no longer knew her sister.

And why would she? It had been ten years since they'd graduated from high school and went off to college in different parts of the country, and they'd barely seen each other in all that time.

They both knew it wasn't home Charlotte had been running from for so long. It was her sister.

For reasons she still didn't understand, from the moment she was old enough to recognize that she was not unique, she had hated having an identical twin.

She'd rather not be here now, but she hadn't been able to say no when her sister had called the day before. Faith had sounded…ragged. This was a woman who'd managed to look and sound serene to everyone, including her father and sister, during the two years her husband was emotionally and physically abusing her. It made Charlotte angry to this day that Faith had put up with so much for so long, and that she hadn't told anyone.

When Charlotte had asked what was wrong, her sister gave a funny, choked laugh. "What isn't? No, I shouldn't say that. Dad and I are alive and…not well, but not dying, either."

"You're not exactly reassuring me," she'd said.

"No. Char, the tractor overturned on Dad."

"Oh, God," she whispered.

"He's…pretty badly hurt. Just bones and… I mean, he'll be okay, he doesn't have a head injury or major internal damage, but he's in traction because one leg and his pelvis were just, um, crushed…." Faith's breath hitched, and she fell silent. Charlotte could hear her breathing. "You know he hasn't been himself since Mom died."

Charlotte closed her eyes. "Yes."

"I'm trying to keep the farm going, but with us in the middle of switching over to the nursery and gift shop and what have you, the only crop we're raising for sale is corn."

Charlotte knew that, too, but only because she'd been told. She'd last been home at Christmas, when the fields would have been mere stubble no matter what crop her dad had sowed the spring before. What Faith was telling her, Charlotte understood, was that the gift shop and nursery, both works in progress, were all that brought in any income—except, of course, for Faith's salary as a kindergarten teacher.

"So I'm off for the summer, but…" Faith's soft voice stumbled again. "I'm having a really hard time keeping up. And, well, I don't know if I told you that Rory started coming around a few months ago."

Rory Hardesty was Faith's bastard of an ex-husband, a local boy who'd seemed to be the solid young man Faith sought until just after she married him. After the marriage was over, she'd confessed that his temper had begun to simmer within the first few months.

Charlotte tensed. "No. You didn't tell me."

"It's not a big deal, mostly. He didn't like the divorce."

Faith was supposed to stay under his thumb and let herself be terrorized into submission.

"But it was final over a year ago."

"I heard he dated a lot the first few months. I guess he figured he'd make me jealous. Lately, I think he's drinking pretty heavily."

"He comes over when he's *drunk?*"

"Not most of the time. Mostly he stops by pretending to be friendly. He says he's sorry for losing his temper a couple of times. He's expecting…hoping, I guess, that I'll take him back."

Faith had been reluctant to tell her the details, but Charlotte knew damn well that Rory had lost his temper a hell of a lot more often than a "couple" of times.

"But lately, I think he *has* been drinking sometimes when he comes by. He hasn't exactly threatened me, but…"

Charlotte was gripping the phone so hard her fingers ached. "But…?"

Her sister said, very softly, "I'm scared, Char. Especially with Dad still in the hospital."

And Faith alone at the farm, with no near neighbors.

"I don't like to ask… I mean, getting time off work probably isn't easy, and coming home isn't exactly what you want to do with your vacation time, but…"

"I was laid off."

This silence was startled. "You lost your job?"

"Last week. Big surprise, with the state of the economy. OpTech laid off a third of their work force. Including me." She'd spent the past week brooding. Sleeping in. Gorging on premium chocolate-mint ice cream. Trying not to wonder how long her savings would pay the mortgage on her San Francisco condominium, never mind buy groceries. Software designers made good money, but she hadn't set as much aside as she should have. Living in the Bay Area was expensive.

More silence. Her sister didn't have to ask why she hadn't called to tell her dearly beloved family. Charlotte had been keeping her distance for too many years now.

No—she'd had no choice at all but to come home.

Seeing Faith now, leaning nonchalantly there in jeans and a T-shirt, her blond hair in a loose braid that fell over her breast, caused an uncomfortable ripple in Charlotte's sense of self. Visits home always did, which was one reason she didn't make more of them.

When she stepped off the Airporter, Faith's eyes widened. "Look at you," she murmured, then smiled shakily and stepped forward. The next moment, the two women were holding each other tight. "I've missed you," Faith said, and Charlotte said, "You should have called sooner," although truthfully she didn't know how she would have responded, had she still held a job.

They parted and studied each other. Charlotte knew what her sister saw: short, sleek, dark hair, two earrings in one lobe and three climbing the other, and a face that was too thin and yet still looked disquietingly like her sister's despite all her effort to make sure it didn't.

Except for that first "Look at you," Faith didn't comment on Charlotte's appearance. Instead, she helped load her luggage into the truck and then said, "Do you want to stop by the hospital before we go home?"

Charlotte nodded. "Yes, please."

Her father was asleep when they walked into his hospital room. He was in the first bed, separated by a curtain from the other bed and the window and any hope of sunshine. Her immediate thought was that he had shrunk. Except for the cast and leg slung up in traction, he didn't seem to have enough bulk underneath the covers. Seeing that, she had a terrible spasm of guilt. He'd aged so much since Mom had died, and she'd hardly noticed.

His eyes opened and she waited while he focused slowly. The dyed hair, new since Christmas, didn't seem to throw him off. "Char." He had to clear a scratchy throat. "I'm sorry you had to come home because of this." He waved toward his leg.

Her eyes blurred, but she smiled for his sake. "I'm sorry you were hurt, but glad to be needed. Did Faith tell you I lost my job?"

He nodded.

"I was feeling sorry for myself. I'm happy to be home."

"Good," he said. His hand groped for hers and squeezed hard, still strong. "Good."

He had to push a button to call the nurse then for his pain meds, and afterward they talked a little but his eyes kept drifting shut. Finally, Charlotte kissed his stubbly cheek and she and Faith left.

Not until they were walking across the parking lot did she say, "He looks…old. And he's only, what, fifty-seven?"

"Fifty-nine," her sister corrected her.

Ashamed that she couldn't even remember how old her own father was, Charlotte said, "Fifty-nine isn't old."

"No." Expression unhappy, Faith unlocked the Blazer. "Since Mom died…I swear Dad has aged four or five years for every one. Maybe, if keeping the farm going hadn't been such a struggle, too…" She stopped; didn't have to finish. *If he'd had* anything *to be glad about, instead of having to deal with his wife's tragic, unnecessary death, his daughter's ugly divorce, his other daughter's increasing distance and the prospect of losing the family farm—if, if, if—he might not look so old.*

While some of the fault was hers, Charlotte knew, most of it wasn't. Losing Mom, that was at the heart of her father's grief, as was the prospect of losing…not just his livelihood, the farm was more than that—it was his heritage, too.

Well, that's what she'd come home for: to help Faith try to salvage that heritage and livelihood both. She had no idea whether it was possible. She'd start by helping keep her sister safe.

Let that son-of-a-bitch Rory stop by when I'm *around,* she thought fiercely. *Just let him.*

IT WAS IMPULSE THAT MADE Gray Van Dusen flick on his signal and make the turn onto the bumpy, hard-packed ground in front of the main barn on the Russell farm. The property held several smaller outbuildings, including a detached garage and a traditional two-story farmhouse painted a pale yellow with white trim. The farm wasn't riverfront—the Stillaguamish looped lazily through the flat valley on the other side of the highway—but it was good land, enriched by centuries of flooding. A man standing here could see the Cascade Mountain foothills to the east and the forested bluff to the north.

A shiny, red monster pickup had pulled in not far ahead of him, raising a cloud of dust that settled on his Prius.

Damn it, he'd washed his car yesterday with his own two hands.

Agriculture was a dying business here in the Stillaguamish River Valley. Farms were too small to compete with agribusiness and, as crop prices continued to drop, local farmers were selling their land to developers. The Russells were more stubborn than most. Their farm, with the big old barn, several outbuildings and a traditional farmhouse, was advantageously placed on the swoop of highway that led from Interstate 5 into the town of West Fork, Washington. These last couple of years, Don Russell and his daughter Faith had begun a conversion from real farming to a seasonal corn maze, pumpkin farm, antique shop, plant nursery and who the hell knew what else.

Gray suspected that the initiative had come from Faith. Don Russell was a taciturn man who, rumor had it, had changed after the death of his wife four years ago. No one thought he would have done battle against the inevitable had one of his two daughters not been so determined to hang on to the family farm.

Gray didn't know the truth of any of this; he couldn't claim to have exchanged more than half a dozen words with Russell. Faith was another matter. He'd taken her out to dinner twice a few months back—once because they were both single and she was pretty, the second time to verify the absence of any spark between them. As far as he was concerned, Faith Russell was a nice woman. He wasn't opposed to nice, but she carried it a little too far. He didn't want to have to be on his best manners for the rest of his life.

Her SUV was parked by the house, her father's pickup by the barn. The newcomer pulled in beside it, and a man in tight jeans and cowboy boots got out and swaggered inside without even turning his head to see who was following him.

Gray parked and went into the barn, too, then waited for his eyes to adjust from the bright sunlight.

The cavernous interior had been carved into aisles and rooms by rough-hewn wood shelving units. Overhead, huge beams and crosspieces held up the roof. A swallow flitted from one beam to another. Perhaps she'd raised a spring brood up there. The doors on the far side of the barn were wide open, letting sunlight stream in and leading to the outside nursery. To Gray's right, half of the barn was devoted to gardening implements, seeds, bagged manure and garden art. To his left, the other half held an organic produce section, and beyond that the antiques. In the center of it all stood a broad counter where homemade jams and jellies were displayed, as well as an old-fashioned cash register.

The only two people in here, besides Gray, were the woman behind the counter and the guy who'd planted himself in front of it, legs apart and his thumbs hooked in his jeans' pockets.

"What in the hell have you done with yourself?" he asked explosively.

The woman—Faith...no, *not* Faith, Gray realized in surprise—gave the guy a look, a flash of vivid blue eyes.

"Had a makeover," she said, not smiling.

"You look like a whore," the jackass sneered. "What're you trying to prove, punchin' holes in yourself?"

"My reasons had nothing to do with you." She leaned forward, her voice low, almost a hiss. "Rory, wife beaters aren't welcome on our land. Consider this a warning. I'll call the cops if you trespass again. Clear?"

From the shadows near the entrance, Gray saw the shoulders bunch and heard a string of obscenities, followed by single name, spat out with venom. "Char." A shrug. "Figures. You'll be gone soon enough. That's what you do, isn't it?" He leaned forward. "This is between Faith and me. Stay out of it."

"Nope." She reached for the telephone that lay on the counter. "Get out of here, Rory. I mean it."

The jackass started forward, not back. Gray cleared his throat. Aware he was imposing enough to give the SOB pause, he strolled farther into the barn. Rory spun around, glared at him, snarled, "I'll be back," and strode toward the open door, his shoulder, not so accidentally, bumping Gray's on the way.

"Last warning," she called after him.

He flipped her off without looking back, then disappeared. The angry roar of the big engine was followed by a swirl of dust that wafted even inside the barn.

"Nice guy," Gray remarked.

She gave a short, sharp laugh and took her hand away from the phone. "Oh, yeah. And getting nicer all the time."

He raised his brows. *Wife beater? Had Faith been married to that bastard?*

She ignored his open curiosity and said conventionally, "May I help you?"

"Faith mentioned she had a sister."

She hadn't said how startlingly similar that sister looked. Both women were taller than average—perhaps five foot seven or eight—and willowy. This sister was thinner yet, though, as if she lived on coffee and nerves but very little food. Her skin was very white, her cheekbones prominent, her nose long and her eyes the blue of a Siamese cat's. Bluer than Faith's, he thought, but perhaps the color was more vivid because of the fire in these eyes. Faith's were the blue of a placid pond rather than the startling blue of the twilight sky above the pyrotechnics of the setting sun.

"Should she have mentioned you?" Faith's sister asked.

He smiled. "Nothing to mention. We're acquainted." He held out his hand. "Gray Van Dusen."

She shook, even as she seemed to be sampling his name. "Gray… Not Graham?"

"Graham," he conceded, letting her hand go with some reluctance, "although I answer to Gray." Did she have any idea how much tension and vitality she'd conveyed, just with that simple grip of her hand?

"The new mayor of West Fork."

"That would be me. Also a partner in Van Dusen and Cullen, Architects."

"Part-time mayor, part-time architect." She sounded amused.

"More like full-time mayor, full-time architect," Gray admitted ruefully. "There's not enough of me to go around."

"And yet you're here to shop for a new shrub or a hundred-year-old dining-room table or, hmm, some blackberry jam?" With the same slender, pale hand he'd enfolded earlier in his own, she lifted a jar from the display and held it out in offering.

Faith's hands did not look like that. They were just as slender and graceful, but also tanned, calloused and nicked.

"Thank you, but no. I actually stopped by to tell Faith that I'm sorry to hear about the accident. And, ah, to talk about traffic."

Her eyes widened. "Traffic? In West Fork?"

"You'd be surprised."

"Maybe not. Faith did say that West Fork is becoming a bedroom community for the east side." She set down the jam jar. "I'm Charlotte. As you can tell, Faith's sister."

He wondered at the wryness in her tone. Had she, once upon a time, played second fiddle to Faith? He simply couldn't imagine, even if Charlotte was the younger.

"He called you Char. Do you go by that?"

"Mostly with family. Rory is Faith's ex, in case you hadn't gathered as much."

"Seems like a real son of a bitch," Gray murmured.

Her voice hardened. "That's how I think of him. Um…this conversation about traffic. Faith's up at the house. Shall I call her?"

He shook his head. "We can have it another time. I stopped on impulse." Following another impulse, he grabbed a different jar of jam. "I prefer blueberry."

Charlotte Russell smiled at him, and he was jolted down to the soles of his feet. "My first chance to use the cash register."

This woman was a mass of contradictions.

That smile, a little sassy but essentially sweet, didn't go with the ice-cold anger she'd used to deal with Rory, the wife beater. If he hadn't been intrigued before, she had him now.

Almost at random, Gray asked, "Do you know how?"

"I'm an expert. I worked at Tastee's while I was in high school."

Like everyone in West Fork, he drove up to the outside window of Tastee's for a burger and fries now and again, or went in for an ice-cream cone. Now amused, he said, "You wore that striped top and the stupid little white hat?"

She rolled her eyes. "I can't tell you how much I hated that hat. Still, it was a job. Faith," she told him, "picked strawberries summers. I wouldn't have been caught dead doing that."

He took out his wallet and paid for the jam, then nodded toward the bright outline of the door. "Walk me out?"

"Why not." She came around the counter, and he saw that below a filmy white, short-sleeved blouse, she wore an aqua-colored, airy, linen skirt that flowed over her hips and thighs and stopped midcalf. Below that, flip-flops bared red-painted toenails. Seeing his gaze, she waved vaguely at her clothes and said, "I flew up here this morning. Haven't had time to change into jeans."

"From where?"

"San Francisco."

"Are you younger, or older?"

The blue eyes flared. "You can't tell?"

He stopped just outside and faced her. "Tell what?"

"We're twins." She was trying to wipe all expression out of her voice but didn't quite succeed. "Identical twins."

"Are you?" Assessing her again, Gray automatically put aside the pang he felt whenever he heard the word *twin*. "I knew right away that you weren't Faith."

"Gee. Black hair? Earrings?" She tugged mockingly at one lobe.

He shrugged. "Rory couldn't."

"That's because he's too self-centered to look very hard at anyone but himself."

Gray suppressed a smile. "You're thinner."

She glanced down at herself. "I guess so. Faith has some muscle tone—she works hard here. I'm just bony. Despite the chocolate-mint ice cream."

He let that pass. "What's inside affects how we look. You and Faith aren't that much alike, are you?"

Charlotte stared at him, her eyes curiously vulnerable. He had the sense that he'd stunned her.

"No. We could…pass for each other, when we

were younger, but inside..." She sighed. "Faith has a gift for serenity that I don't."

"You seem...stronger," he chose to say, instead of telling her she had a fire her sister lacked.

But she was shaking her head before he finished. "No. She was here for Mom and Dad, she withstood an awful marriage, she's fighting to save the farm—and, so far, winning. Me, I had a job and a condo and no one else to worry about. In comparison to me, Faith is an Amazon."

He picked the most important three words out of this speech. "No one else?"

She flushed, and he smiled. *Good,* he thought.

Then he wondered at her choice of verb tense. *Had* implied that she no longer had a job, or perhaps the condo. Or both.

"How long do you plan to be here?" he asked.

"I don't know. Depends how quick Dad recovers, how much of a nuisance Rory turns out to be."

Gray frowned. "Has Faith called the police or tried to get a protection order?"

Charlotte shook her head. "I don't think so. We'll talk about it." She eyed him. "Is this traffic thing something I should know about?"

"Depends how involved you get with the farm. I'm just worrying about your customers pulling out right onto the highway, especially on this curve here. Somebody misjudges distance or speed, and we'll have multiple fatalities."

"What do you suggest?" she shot back. "We sell the farm? You know a housing development will replace it. Then you'll have that traffic to contend with."

"Developers," he pointed out, "are required to mitigate traffic problems. Maybe pay for a left-turn lane, and to add one to give cars pulling out room to accelerate."

"We can't afford anything like that." She stared him down. "Why don't you go to the state and ask for a lower speed limit, or a center lane?"

"Because that would take years, expensive studies and bureaucratic obstacles beyond either of our imaginations. Meantime, people are going to die."

"You don't want us running a retail business right off the highway."

"I'm not happy about it." Or about alienating her before he'd even had a chance to ask her to dinner. "I've got a couple of ideas, though."

She gave her head a quick shake. "You'll want to talk to Faith, then. With Dad so woozy, she's the decision-maker. I'm here to be a minion."

His mouth quirked. "A minion?"

"Yeah, you know. A helper. A floor-mopper, cashier. I suspect she'll have me making jam and driving the tractor before I know it. A nurse, too, I suppose, when Dad comes home." She made a face at that. "Although Faith would be *much* better at nursing than I would."

"Because of her gift for serenity."

"And my impatience with my fellow human beings."

"What do you do for a living?" he asked.

"Design software." She pressed her lips together, opened them as if to say something else, then decided not to.

A solitary occupation. He wondered what kind of software she designed. Word processing? Financial? Something arcane that made computers run faster or repelled viruses? Games?

Probably not games.

He glanced over his shoulder and saw that a van was pulling in. A family would shortly be spilling out of it.

"Nice to meet you, Charlotte Russell," he said with a nod. "I'll see you again soon."

For the first time, her expression seemed to turn shy. Her tone, in contrast, was flip. "Like I told you, Faith's the one you want to talk to."

"Oh, I don't know," he said. "I think I'd enjoy talking to you."

She gave him a look that, if he wasn't mistaken, held alarm.

The van came to a stop. When the side door

slid open, at least four kids scrambled out, as well as two women from the front seats.

She said only, "I'll tell Faith you were here," and greeted the customers, leading the way into the barn.

Not until Gray was alone did he say softly, "Faith's not the one I want."

Want, he thought, was a mild word for what he felt for a woman he'd barely met. One who was prickly in personality and too skinny. He'd liked how fierce she had been in her sister's defense, but her smile was what had really gotten to him. Her smile, and the vulnerability he'd seen in her eyes.

But he'd seen plenty of beautiful smiles, and had met his share of women who looked as if they needed somebody to take care of them. So why, this time, did he feel as if he'd been sucker punched?

Frowning, he got in his car. By the time he backed out, he was already thinking about how soon he could stop by the Russell farm again.

CHAPTER TWO

FAITH SAT AT THE KITCHEN TABLE cutting circles out of calico fabric, each of which would dress up a jar of jam or jelly. Her scissors followed the lines she'd traced on the fabric with a quilter's marker, using a saucer as the pattern. The fabric would be held taut across the top of the jar, then flare into a ruffle below the ring. The work to make the Russell Family Farm jams and jellies look fancier—more worthy of gift-giving—was worth it, she thought.

Out of the corner of her eye she watched Char use tongs to lift sterilized jars from a large pot of boiling water. Raspberry jam bubbled on the other larger burner. She'd looked aghast when Faith tried to give her the job of cutting fabric.

"Don't you remember what a disaster I made out of every sewing project I ever tried?"

"Um...yes." Faith actually had forgotten. Although how, she couldn't imagine. The apron Char had once made Mom for Christmas had been... Well. She cleared her throat. "This is just tracing and cutting."

Backing away from the proffered fabric yardage Faith had held in outstretched hands, Char said firmly, "I'd a thousand times rather make jam."

The Russells had hardly ever bought fruit or vegetables; they grew and preserved their own. By the time the girls were ten years old, they could can green beans or whip up a batch of apple jelly or blackberry jam without supervision. Faith had always been more eager to learn chores like that—she'd liked just about everything to do with farm life better than her sister had. But, obviously, the lessons had stuck even for Char, who'd been able to jump in without hesitation this morning, leaving her sister to water potted plants in the nursery and then start the finicky work of tracing circles.

It was wretchedly hot today, and even with windows standing open and a rotating fan running nonstop, it was at least ninety degrees in the kitchen. Poor Char, who had gotten sunburned yesterday helping pick the berries, had lost all resemblance to the chic urban woman who had arrived two days ago. Despite the fact that she wore only shorts and a tank top, she was sweating and kept having to reach for a kitchen towel to wipe her face. Her hair poked up in damp tufts and stuck to her forehead and temples. Forget makeup. She hadn't bothered with earrings this morning, either.

She was trying; Faith had to give her that. No, the fact that she was here at all was amazing enough.

Be grateful for that.

Faith was trying, too—to be grateful, that is. She was trying not to hate the fact that Char could hardly stand to look at her.

Char was handling this stay she'd felt obliged to make by sticking to business. They talked about Dad and how they'd take care of him once he came home, about the corn grown almost tall enough to open the maze to the public, about how much jam would sell and about whether they could afford to increase the hours of the teenage girl Faith had recently hired to help out part-time.

And Rory. Char wanted to talk about him, too. Faith was the one sliding away from that conversation because she knew perfectly well that Char would want to take action that Faith didn't believe was justified. It wasn't as though she still loved him; he'd killed anything she'd once felt for him a long time ago, but she did have memories of the Rory she once *had* loved. And he'd give up eventually on his own, wouldn't he? When he couldn't get a rise out of her either way?

But that was one of the many ways she and

Charlotte differed. Char's instinct was always to come up swinging. Literally, when they were kids—Char was the only girl at their elementary school who was called in to the principal's office not just once, but *twice* for brawling. Both times she was defending Faith, who hadn't seen any need for defense.

Char, she knew, would have booted Rory out on his butt the first time he questioned why she was late and who she'd been talking to. She wouldn't have waited until he hit her, and she'd never have given him second and third and fourth and fifth chances. In Rory's case, Char would have been right. As it turned out, he *hadn't* deserved any of those chances. But people often did, in Faith's experience, so was it really so awful that she'd wanted to believe in the man she had loved?

She should try to articulate how she felt to her sister. After all, she was the one who had begged Char to come and who had admitted that Rory scared her. But Charlotte-at-a-distance and Charlotte-actually-here were not at all the same sister. It was a little like the way Faith saw Rory, as if he were a layer of transparencies on the overhead projector in her classroom, and she could peel a few off and there would be the Rory she'd first known.

The Charlotte she'd first known was her twin. Her other half. They'd curled in the womb together, slept side by side in the same crib, shared toys and clothes and their mother's arms. They'd never needed words to understand each other.

Which made it all the sadder that now they needed words and couldn't bring themselves to speak them.

She had never understood why Char had hated having an identical twin. Faith only felt whole when Charlotte was near. They reflected each other, yes, but they each had their own strengths and weaknesses. They complemented each other.

That's not how Char felt about it. It was as if…as if Faith's very existence lessened her. One of Faith's earliest memories was of Charlotte screaming and struggling because Mom was trying to make her wear the pretty pink parka that was just like Faith's. They couldn't have been more than three years old. Charlotte had howled, over and over again, "I won't! It's *hers!* I won't!" The scene was colored, in Faith's memory, by her own bewilderment.

Somehow, Faith always forgot. Each time her sister came home, she expected that they would read each others' minds from the first glance, not be unable to meet each other's eyes.

Wouldn't you think that after all these years, she would have gotten over it? Faith thought.

Moved on? It was her own fault that it hurt so much every time Char came home and Faith saw again how much her sister wished they weren't twins. Maybe even that the egg had remained undivided and only one of them had been born in the first place.

What was, was.

She stared blindly down at the scissors she held in her hand.

Why have I spent a lifetime feeling as if she's a necessary part of who I am, while all she's ever wanted is to amputate the part of her that's me?

The great, unanswerable question.

She jumped up. "Why did I ever think decorating jars of jam was a good idea? Ugh. Let me help you."

Her twin actually grinned at her. "Yeah, why *did* you? And pretty please—I'm losing control here."

Ridiculously warmed by the flash of camaraderie, Faith took the tongs from her hand and said, "Do something about the jam. It looks like lava about ready to head for the sea."

"Boy, this is fun," Charlotte muttered—but not as if she *really* minded spending the day in the hot kitchen with her sister.

She'd be foolish to hope for too much, Faith cautioned herself. Every time Charlotte came home, Faith let herself imagine that *this* time they might rediscover the bond that had tied them together as children despite Char's discomfiture. *This* time, Char might open herself to her sister, decide they could be friends at least.

But Faith had been hoping for a long time, and it hurt to be disappointed. Char was here out of a sense of obligation, that was all, and expecting more was asking to be hurt once again.

Faith had sworn, when she left Rory, that she'd never invite that kind of pain again.

So don't.

THE TEMPERATURE NEVER USED TO get up into the nineties, not when she'd lived here. Summers had just plain gotten hotter. As humid as it was in the Puget Sound area, today had been close to unendurable. Thank God for indoor plumbing—Charlotte had taken three showers today—and for nightfall. It didn't stay hot at night here summers the way it did in, say, Chicago where Charlotte had landed her first postgrad job.

It was now past midnight, and she'd tried turning out the light and going to bed, but sleep was eluding her.

Why she hadn't tumbled onto her bed at 8:00 p.m. and conked out, she had no idea. Well, not at eight—in August, the sun didn't set until nine-thirty or so and she'd never been able to sleep with daylight outside the window. On the other hand, she hadn't worked this hard physically in ten years or more, and she should be exhausted.

She was, in one way—she *hurt*. Having made a habit out of hitting the gym at least four days a week, she'd kidded herself that she was in decent shape. Ha! *Not*. The damn sunburn wasn't helping, and it was her own fault. Charlotte had forgotten how white her skin was. Sunburn wasn't much of a problem in the foggy Bay Area, especially since a half-hour jog was about the longest she was ever outside.

But aside from the physical aches and pains, she felt weirdly energized by the past couple of days. It seemed hard work suited her, or at least that she'd needed some to pull her out of the funk she'd been in when Faith called. Picking berries, weeding the perennial beds that wrapped the barn and making jam had seemed so…real, compared to what she did normally with her life. She'd been ridiculously proud of what she had wrought, when she admired the rows and rows of jars sitting on the kitchen countertop. She was going to enjoy selling *her* jam.

Too bad she hadn't made any blueberry.

She was too smart to waste a thought on Gray Van Dusen, part-time mayor, part-time architect. But she kept doing it anyway.

He was a good architect, according to Faith, and probably a good mayor, although he hadn't been on the job long enough yet to have gotten far with West Fork's many problems. He was also an incredibly sexy man, which was why she kept having to nudge him out of her head.

He wasn't her usual type, which was a thin, intense geek. Funny, because even in high school that was her type. Jocks *so* didn't interest her.

Gray would have been a jock. Although, in fairness, she suspected he was exceptionally smart, too. He was…not huge, but probably six feet tall or so, broad-shouldered and lean in the way of a man who probably ran for exercise, maybe still played fast-pitch or basketball but wasn't interested in the tedium of weight lifting. His hair was just a little longer than she suspected some of his constituents would like, a brown that was streaked bronze and gold by the sun. Calm, gray eyes—what else, considering his name? A face that should have been ordinary-handsome, but was somehow more than that, maybe because his nose looked like it had been broken at some point, maybe because of those hooded eyes that were thoughtful but also tinged with humor. She didn't see Mayor Van Dusen as being volatile. He'd be the kind to mull over his options for a good long while before he made decisions.

And stubborn. She just knew he'd be stubborn.

The traffic thing, according to Faith, was an example. He'd made three visits now to discuss it, including one yesterday. Charlotte had seen him walking into the barn and had slipped out the back. Instinct had told her to evade him, jolting her into motion before she even knew what or whom she was running from.

It was just common sense, she told herself. Letting herself be attracted to a man in West Fork wasn't logical, considering how short her stay was likely to be.

She probably hadn't had to bother slipping out today. If he'd had traffic on his mind, it was Faith he wanted anyway, not her. But somehow, she didn't quite believe he'd been motivated to stop by the Russell farm a second day in a row because he was determined to talk about cars merging onto Highway 519. No, he'd been interested in her. The way he'd gently suggested she walk him out to his car, and she'd obliged without a second thought... If she gave him any toehold at all, he'd be as relentless as a tiny, ceaseless drip of water that eventually hollowed out granite.

Which was why she was *not* going to think about him, and would continue to slip out one door when he came in the other. He'd get the message, and she wouldn't have to bother for long.

Without turning on her bedroom light,

Charlotte got out of bed, slipped on the shorts she'd worn that evening and groped with her toes for her flip-flops. Because of the heat, she'd worn panties and a tank top to bed, so she was now decent. She had a sudden craving to step outside, savor the cool night air, maybe walk away from the house, listen to the silence, and tip her head back to see the stars in a way she never could in a city.

Home smelled different, too. So, okay, part of what she'd smell was manure, but that beat automobile exhaust, didn't it?

Faith's bedroom was right across the hall, where it had been ever since they'd turned ten and Charlotte had insisted on having her own room. Faith, she'd known, was unhappy when she moved out and started shutting her bedroom door, but she had needed that space and privacy with a desperation she couldn't explain, that felt like a fever reaching dangerous heights. She hadn't wanted to hurt Faith, but she would if that was the only way she could *separate* herself. She'd been as miserable as if they were conjoined, condemned to share a life unless they chose the huge risk of surgical sunderance. Charlotte had read up on identical twins when she was eight or nine, and she remembered staring with fascination and horror at pictures of conjoined twins.

I could not bear it, she'd thought, and meant it.

She would have chosen in a heartbeat to have the surgery to divide them, even if she didn't survive it. Her need had been that great, and that irrational.

Today was the first time in years that she could remember talking to Faith and laughing and forgetting, for moments at a time, that they were more than just sisters. She'd looked at Faith's face without seeing a reflection of her own.

Maybe, at last, her efforts to define herself were working. Or maybe she had just put aside her discomfiture because Faith—and Dad—needed her.

And maybe, she thought with a twinge, it had something to do with Gray Van Dusen, who had been surprised when she told him she and Faith were identical twins.

You and Faith aren't that much alike, are you?

No, she had thought sadly; Faith's the strong one, and I'm the coward. Running, always running.

What she didn't know was where she thought she was going. Just lately, it was a question she'd begun to ask herself. A need for the answer just might be one reason she hadn't started job hunting more aggressively.

From long habit, she skipped the third step from the bottom, which always squeaked. Not that she was sneaking out, exactly, but she was in a solitary mood.

She'd put her questions out of her mind, too. Right now, she didn't want to think about why she felt something was missing from the life she'd carved for herself. She just wanted to *be*.

Rather than go out the front door, which looked toward the highway, Charlotte went through the kitchen. Rows and rows of jars still sat along the countertop, the glass reflecting glints of moonlight falling through the kitchen windows. Without turning on the overhead or porch light, she stepped out the back door, the screen door creaking as she let it snap shut behind her.

The night air was as cool as she'd hoped, but with her first breath, she smelled smoke. Her head turned sharply. What was burning? Even as she hurried toward the corner of the house, her mind tried to find a good reason for a midnight fire. A woodstove? Not on a hot August day. Slash burning on cleared land, even just a neighbor who'd cut out blackberry vines. No, she'd seen the sign announcing a burn ban out in front of the fire station. And besides, she hadn't smelled a fire when she'd gone to bed at ten or so. She rounded the house and stopped dead.

Flames crawled up the side of the barn.

Charlotte gasped, whirled around and ran back the way she'd come, stumbling once and barely noticing the pain. She flung herself up the couple of steps and through the kitchen.

At the bottom of the stairs, she bellowed, "Faith! Wake up! The barn's on fire!" She wheeled again and raced for the kitchen, grabbed the phone and dialed 9-1-1. "Barn's on fire," she gasped and gave the address before dropping the telephone and bolting back outside. Heart pounding, she ran.

The fire had already leaped higher, toward the roof, but it wasn't huge yet. Oh, God—as old as this barn was, the wood was the perfect tinder. She'd done the watering tonight, and knew exactly where she'd dropped the nozzle and where the faucet was. She turned it on full blast and aimed the nozzle toward the barn wall. Even when she pulled the hose out taut, the stream barely reached the fire, and she could see that it wouldn't be enough, but she kept spraying, above, around, below.

The house lights had sprung on behind her, and Faith wasn't a minute behind her, running in some kind of thin nightgown and flip-flops like Charlotte's.

"You called 9-1-1?" she yelled as she ran past, and Charlotte yelled back, "Yes!"

There was another faucet round back, Charlotte remembered, but a minute, two minutes, passed before a second stream of water joined hers. Faith had probably had to hook up a hose.

The scream of the siren wasn't far behind. They were lucky, so lucky, that the volunteer fire station was less than half a mile away. The first truck roared in, the headlights spotlighting Charlotte but not her sister, who was behind the barn. She kept the stream of water aimed at the barn even as the firemen ran toward her pulling a hose that made hers look like a child's toy.

"Get back, ma'am, please get back!" she was told, and she let the nozzle fall from her shaking hand.

Adrenaline roaring through her, she backed away and kept backing until she felt mown grass under her feet again. She was hugging herself when Faith reached her and they grabbed each other and held on, neither of them looking away from the fiery scene and the eerie sight of water soaring in great arcs to cascade down over their 100-year-old barn and the licking flames.

"Oh, no, oh, no, oh, no," Faith moaned.

"Everything inside will be wet," Charlotte whispered.

Faith whimpered and buried her face briefly against her sister's neck, then lifted her head again as if she couldn't stand not to watch her dreams burn.

The smell now was stomach-turning: smoke

and the wet, charred odor of a campfire doused in water. Something else, too, Charlotte thought in one corner of her mind. Gasoline, maybe from the fire trucks?

The fire sank back quickly, not big enough to defy a drowning. Faith and Charlotte clung to each other and kept watching as firemen prowled outside and stepped through the hole burned in the side of the barn to check, presumably, for hidden embers.

Eventually, one of the firemen, bulky in a cumbersome yellow suit, crossed the yard.

"Faith, is that you?"

"Yes, and Charlotte, too. Char, you remember Tim Crawford?"

She nodded. "Of course I do. I'm…um, really glad you got here so quick, Tim."

He'd been one—two?—years ahead of them, and best friends with Jay Bridges, quarterback, whom Faith had gone with her freshman year. Charlotte had liked Tim better than Jay, not that either of them were her type.

"We're confident we've got the fire out," Tim was saying. "It's real lucky one of you noticed it before the whole barn was engaged."

"I couldn't sleep," Charlotte said. "I was just going to come out and sit on the back steps and admire the stars. But I smelled smoke the moment I got outside."

"Lucky," he said again, nodding. "Five, ten more minutes, you'd have lost the barn."

A shudder ran through Faith. Charlotte tightened her arms around her sister.

"How do you think it started?" Charlotte asked.

"It's arson," he said bluntly. "Can't you smell the gasoline? And I know it's hard to see the smoke at night like this, but it was black. I'm going to make sure someone is out here in the morning to talk to you about it."

"Can we, um, look inside?" Faith asked shakily.

Sounding kind, he said, "Why don't you wait until daylight? Get a good night's sleep. Didn't look like that much damage to me."

"Oh." Faith nodded, and kept nodding. "Oh, okay."

"Thanks, Tim," Charlotte said, and steered her sister toward the house. Behind them, the volunteer firemen were reeling in their hoses and climbing aboard the two trucks. Engines started before the two women reached the house.

In the kitchen, Charlotte said, "I don't know about you, but I want a drink. Do you have anything?"

"Daddy keeps some bourbon up top of the refrigerator, but I'd settle for tea." Faith sank into a kitchen chair as if her legs had just failed her. "In a minute. When I can stand up again."

Charlotte shook her head. "I'll make it." She thought wistfully about a slug of the bourbon but instead got down two mugs, plopped in tea bags, filled them with water and stuck them in the microwave. One minute later, and the water was hot. Without asking Faith, she added more sugar than she liked to one of the mugs, then carried them both to the table.

"Thank you." Faith smiled wanly at her. Soot streaked her face, which was paler than it ought to be considering she had a good tan. Her thin nightgown had gotten a blast of water at some point and clung revealingly to her. Below the hem, her feet were filthy.

Charlotte looked down and realized she looked just as awful. Her feet were not only filthy, but one of her toes was also bloody. She had a vague memory of stubbing it. "You know I had three showers today?" she said. "And now I'm going to have to have a fourth?"

"It's tomorrow now," her sister pointed out. She stirred her tea, then lifted out the bag. "So this won't be your fourth shower of today, it'll be your first shower of tomorrow. No, today."

Suddenly they were both giggling.

"Oh, Lord," Faith finally said on a sigh, her hand pressed to her stomach. "I was sound asleep.

I never would have woken up. It really is a miracle you happened to go outside."

Charlotte met her sister's eyes. "Rory was awfully mad the other day."

"It could've just been a teenager. Why would Rory do something like this? He wants me back. He'd have to know that would blow any chance…."

Charlotte set down her mug hard. "Does he *have* a chance?"

"No!" Faith glared at her. "How can you even ask me that?"

"You're the one who just implied…"

"I did not! I was trying to explain how *he* thinks!"

Charlotte let out a frustrated breath. "When you called, you sounded like he'd been angry lately when he came around. And he was nasty from the minute he walked into the barn day before yesterday."

"There's a big difference between…"

God give her patience. "Yes, there is. But if he's getting angry, it's because he's realized he doesn't have another chance. You thought he'd just go away once he realized that, didn't you?"

Stricken, Faith finally closed her mouth and nodded, just once.

"But when you were married, he got violent

every time he thought he was losing control of you."

"Yes," her sister whispered.

"Maybe after he put you in the hospital he was ashamed of himself for a little while. Maybe he thought if he gave you time you'd forgive him eventually. But if he's finally realized you aren't going to, do you really think he's not going to make some…I don't know, some parting gesture?"

Head bowed, gaze fixed on her tea, Faith looked…broken. "I don't know. I guess I was more afraid he'd get mad and hit me. This seems so…sneaky."

"He must know how badly you want to keep the farm going, for Dad's sake, and because it's ours."

She heard herself and thought, *Ours? Where had that come from?*

Faith looked up, eyes red-rimmed and cheeks dirty. "This would have been one of the worst things he could do to me."

Charlotte didn't say anything. She didn't have to.

After a moment of silence, Faith said, "There are other possibilities. It could have just been random vandalism. Or… You know how Angie just started a couple of weeks ago?"

"Yes, but what does that have to do…?"

Faith interrupted. "I had a boy who worked for me before Angie. I caught him stealing money from the till and had to fire him."

Charlotte blinked. "You didn't tell me that."

"He claimed it was the first time he stole anything, but I didn't believe him."

"Really? You didn't think he'd learned his lesson and would be grateful and loyal if you kept him on?"

Faith sprang to her feet. "That's enough! You don't know me at all anymore. I will not let you treat me as if there's anything wrong with believing my husband loved me enough to change."

Shame flooded Charlotte. She rose, too, facing her sister across the small kitchen table. "You're right. I'm…really sorry."

Faith just looked at her, then turned and walked out of the kitchen. A moment later, footsteps went up the stairs and then Charlotte heard a door shut.

"Why did I say that?" she asked the silent room. The awful thing was, she knew the answer, which made her feel even worse.

CHAPTER THREE

GRAY VAN DUSEN WAS THE first visitor come morning, which somehow did not surprise Charlotte. He was probably kept well informed about any exciting events in West Fork. She imagined him sipping his morning coffee while he perused an e-mail list of every fire and police call made in the previous twenty-four hours.

Faith had slept later than Charlotte. She was standing in the kitchen sipping her coffee and gazing out the window toward the barn when she heard the shower start upstairs. It surprised her, making her realize that she hadn't heard Faith take a shower last night, either before or after her own. Had her twin really crawled into bed still grubby and covered in soot? Charlotte felt a pang of renewed guilt. If Faith had done something as alien to her nature as that, guess whose fault it was?

It would have been worse if I weren't here at all, she reminded herself. *Then the barn would have burned down.*

After recognizing the distinctive shape of

Gray's black Prius, Charlotte decided it wouldn't be fair to hide out until Faith came downstairs. She'd need coffee and breakfast. Charlotte had already had both.

Resigned but wary, she went out the back door as she had last night and walked toward the barn. Gray had circled it and was staring at the burned portion when she reached him.

He was dressed up today, perhaps for meetings, but had left his suitcoat in the car. He wore gray slacks with a narrow black belt, a white shirt and black dress shoes that weren't benefiting from the dust. The white shirt emphasized the breadth of his shoulders, and from behind she admired the fit of the slacks.

Yeah, right. She'd have been looking at his butt even if he'd worn wrinkled khaki.

"You must have heard about our fire," she said.

His head turned, his thoughtful gray eyes taking in her cropped chinos and snug-fitting, royal blue T-shirt. She wondered whether he was inventorying her clothing, or admiring the fit. So to speak. His appraisal made warmth rise in her cheeks, which annoyed her.

"Yes." His expression was grave. "I'm told you were awake, or the barn would have been a goner."

"It's August," she said.

He grunted. "We haven't had any rain in almost two months. And this barn is an old-timer, isn't it? Imagine how dry that wood must be."

They both flicked involuntary glances at the charred side and the gaping hole the fire had burned.

"I hear it was arson," Gray said.

"So Tim Crawford told us. Do you know Tim?"

He nodded. "Crawford is my informant. How is Faith?"

"Upset." *And I made her more upset.* Charlotte sighed. "I don't know any more to tell you at this point. We haven't even gone in yet to see how much damage there is. I'm waiting for Faith. We were both tired and slept in."

"Are you insured?"

"I don't know. We were still worrying about who set the fire when we went to bed. I thought talking about finances could wait for morning." She added quickly, "We haven't told Dad yet, either, needless to say. I hope no one else does."

He gave her a dry look. "I won't dash off to the hospital before I go to city hall."

"I didn't mean…" She closed her eyes briefly. "I'm sorry. It just struck me how Dad will fuss if he hears."

"Can't say I blame him." Gray was silent for

a moment, then said, "I'm going to worry about you two now."

"If anybody's the target, it's Faith. Not me."

"But you're in the middle of things, and I don't see you as a woman to step aside from a threat."

"You don't know me."

"Am I wrong?" he asked quietly.

Of course he wasn't. She'd gotten in trouble more than once in her life because of her refusal to back down. But how did he know that about her? It bothered Charlotte that he'd read her so accurately on such short acquaintance.

"There must be other citizens of West Fork you need to worry about."

His eyes rested warmly on her face. "Ah, but there's something about you, Charlotte Russell. If I'm thinking about you anyway, I might as well worry a little bit."

Then don't think about me, she wanted to say. *Please, please don't.*

It was bad enough that *she* had already caught herself thinking about him more than she should. Gray stirred something in her that wasn't simple attraction, which she could handle. No, this was more like...what she felt every time she looked at her sister, Charlotte realized in dismay. A kind of fear, as if, like Faith, he could breach her inner guard.

Which was ridiculous. She was making too much of this. She couldn't afford to get involved with a guy locally, that's all. She'd steer clear of Gray for that reason, not let herself imagine… something more significant.

He'd been watching her closely, his expression grave. Now he said, in a low voice that felt like a caress, "Charlotte…"

They both heard another car pulling in, and the slam of the house screen door at nearly the same moment. Gray didn't finish whatever he'd intended to say and Charlotte, her pulse having leapt, told herself she was glad. Their gazes touched one more time; he'd wiped all the intensity from his expression, leaving his face impassive.

"Faith," he said, nodding, as Charlotte's sister neared. And then, "Wheeler."

Charlotte looked to see a man coming toward them. Recognizing the traditional blue uniform of the West Fork department she realized he was a police officer, not a fire marshal.

Faith looked better than Charlotte felt; she'd resumed her usual mask of serenity, though it couldn't possibly be genuine this morning. Her still damp hair hung loose over her shoulders, and she seemed to have taken the time to apply some makeup. She greeted the mayor with a friendly smile and murmured, "Sorry I slept in, Char," before also facing the policeman.

He was at least Gray's height, perhaps an inch or two taller, and equally broad-shouldered. Charlotte guessed him to be a little older than Gray, perhaps pushing forty. He was dark-haired, dark-eyed and saturnine, and all the sexier for a face that looked…lived in. No, more than that: battered, with a long-since-healed scar that stretched from one cheek to his temple.

He had been staring at Faith. Charlotte saw the moment when color delicately tinted her sister's face and her eyes shied from his. Apparently recognizing that he'd made her uncomfortable, he inclined his head at her before looking at Charlotte.

He blinked, glanced again at Faith, then back at her.

"Yes, we're twins," she said.

He cleared his throat. "So I see. Sorry if I gaped. Ah…I'm Chief Wheeler. Ben Wheeler. I wanted to talk to you about last night's fire."

"Yes, of course," Charlotte agreed. "Do you mind if we take a quick look inside the barn first?"

"Of course not."

Gray accompanied the police chief and the two women inside, although Charlotte saw him steal a look at his watch first. She remembered him saying that he felt as if he was trying to hold down two full-time jobs, and this visit didn't fall under the definition of either. City officials concerned themselves with zoning and taxes, streets and traffic, not minor instances of crime.

This was the third time he'd stopped by in four days. His persistence caused a flutter of panic in her chest. She had been trying to convince herself that he wasn't coming back because of her, but now she couldn't.

Ah, but there's something about you, Charlotte Russell.

Determined to ignore him, she stuck with Faith as they walked into the barn. But—damn it—all the determination in the world didn't seem to do any good. With every cell in her body, she *felt* him right behind her.

They could see immediately how lucky they'd been. The fire had been set in the nursery area, and just inside had been garden art and wrought-iron trellises that were designed to withstand water, at least. A rack of gardening gloves had burned and melted, and the herbal wreaths hung on the batten-board walls had been consumed, but that was the extent of the loss.

Faith turned to Charlotte with a glowing smile and gave her a big hug. "Not that much water got in! Oh, thank goodness! I was so afraid to find out."

Charlotte hugged her back. Her own relief surprised her. "It could have been way worse," she agreed. "Though we'll have to find someone to replace that stretch of barn wall, unless you're a better carpenter than I am."

Backing away, Faith grimaced. "I can do some things, but probably not that. I'll have to think about who to call." She stopped and turned to the police chief. "Gosh, you probably have to ask us questions, don't you?"

"I'm afraid so," he said apologetically.

"I need to run," Gray said. "Uh…were you insured, Faith?"

The strain showed on her face for the first time this morning. "I'm not sure. I'll have to talk to Dad and dig out the paperwork. I know we haven't insured the retail inventory, but Dad must have had some coverage on the structure as a working farm."

"Very likely," he said. "Give me a call. I might know someone who can do the work."

"Okay." She smiled at him. "Thanks, Gray."

His gaze flicked to Charlotte. "Will you walk me out?"

She hesitated, even though a part of her was glad that he'd asked. "Uh…sure," she finally said. Perhaps he wanted to tell her something out of Faith's hearing.

"Wheeler," he said with a nod. "Faith."

As they stepped out into the sunlight, he asked, "This place paying its way?"

Surprised at his choice of topic, Charlotte admitted, "I don't think so." She offered a twisted smile. "I have a suspicion you won't have to keep fussing about the traffic issue."

"Are you going to be able to make a difference?"

"With the farm? Heck, no! I can help take care of Dad, and maybe defend Faith from Rory, but the closest thing to retail experience I have was my part-time job at Tastee's. Is there something we can do to draw more people, bring in more money? I can't think of anything."

His nod was unsurprised. "I suppose you're wishing you were back in front of a computer."

She opened her mouth to agree and realized it would be a lie. She did like her work, but she hadn't missed it since arriving home. "Well, I'm not cut out to be a farmer or run a country store," she said instead, which *wasn't* a lie.

"Charlotte—" Gray stopped and looked past her, and she turned to see the police chief and her sister walking out of the barn to join them.

"Still here?" Wheeler said, faintly mocking.

Gray made a sound in his throat that Charlotte couldn't interpret and said, "I'm going." His eyes meeting hers again, he said quietly, "Take care, okay?"

"I will," she agreed, her own voice low, as if this promise was private. The idea quickened her pulse, but he was turning away, getting into his car.

A moment later, he'd backed out and driven off.

She was pathetic enough to want to watch until his Prius was out of sight. Instead, she faced the police chief and, somewhat hastily, suggested, "Why don't we talk in the kitchen? We could at least sit down and have a cup of coffee."

"I'd appreciate that," he agreed, in a deep, quiet voice.

She was less sure inviting him in had been a good idea when she realized how he seemed to shrink the farmhouse kitchen by his mere presence. Faith lost all animation once the three of them sat down and he began to ask questions.

He concentrated on Charlotte, once Faith told him she hadn't heard or seen a thing until her sister yelled up the stairs to her.

"Did it cross your mind as you ran over to the barn that the arsonist might still be there watching?" he asked, those dark eyes steady on her face.

A chill crept up her spine, raising goose bumps as it went. "I…didn't even think about it being arson," she said. "Not until the firefighter told us. I did notice the smell of gasoline, but not until the fire truck had already pulled in, so I thought…" She trailed off with the unpleasant realization that someone *could* have been watching. There had been moonlight, yes, but he could have stood in the shadow of the garage or one of the smaller outbuildings and smiled at the sight of his fire leaping toward the barn roof. Had he been angry when he saw her and then Faith, or had he enjoyed their desperate fight to save the old barn?

Faith looked horrified, too.

"Oh, Char," she whispered.

Charlotte reached out a hand to her. "It might not have been Rory."

She couldn't remember the last time they'd clasped hands like this. Of course their hands were identical, with long, slender fingers. A few days ago, hers would have been paler, her nails manicured and polished. But now, she was already starting to tan, and a bandage wrapped one finger burned when she stirred the jam. Both of them had acquired scratches thanks to the berry vines.

Charlotte gave her sister's hand a squeeze and then let it go.

The police chief was waiting politely, his dark eyes taking in more, she suspected, than she or her sister would have liked.

"Rory?" he inquired.

Faith bit her lip and gazed at the tabletop as if the pattern of the blue gingham cloth fascinated her. “My ex-husband. Um…Rory Hardesty.”

He had taken out a small notebook when he first sat down, and now carefully wrote down the name. “I take it the divorce wasn’t amicable?”

Faith’s hair swung when she shook her head.

He watched her for a moment, then raised his brows at Char.

“The divorce was final a year ago,” she explained. “He was…abusive.” Faith didn’t react in any way, so she continued, “He’s been coming around lately.”

“How often?”

“Once or twice a week,” Faith said softly.

The intense, dark gaze turned back to Charlotte.

“Faith thinks he has been drunk a few of the times. He clearly wants her back. Sometimes he’s cajoling, sometimes he’s angry. Rory was angry a lot.”

She might have imagined the way his expression hardened, but she didn’t think so.

“Our dad was injured recently when the tractor overturned. He’s still in the hospital. I’m just here for a visit, to help out until he’s on his feet again. My first day home, Tuesday, Rory came by and mistook me for Faith. He harangued me for looking like a slut. Apparently he doesn’t appreciate multiple piercings." She fingered one of her ears. "Perhaps fortunately, Gray walked in right then and Rory stormed out. I'm afraid this fire is exactly the kind of thing he'd do." She paused. "Faith doesn't agree."

Her sister raised her head. "Rory's never done anything criminal."

"Putting you in the hospital wasn't a crime?" Charlotte asked.

"Well…not in the same way." She turned a look of appeal on Chief Wheeler. "It's just that I think there are likelier possibilities. Gosh, this could have just been garden-variety vandalism, couldn't it?"

His voice sounded gentle, considering its deep, rough tenor. "Yes. That's a good possibility. Especially if you've annoyed any teenagers lately."

Almost eagerly, Faith explained about the boy she'd fired just a few weeks back. When she got to the point of giving his name, though, the eagerness had dwindled. "Sean. Sean Coffey. The thing is, I really think he's basically a nice kid. He's on the football team, and his dad is a teacher. Not at my school, at Roosevelt Elementary. And I did catch Sean red-handed. He couldn't complain that I was being unfair."

"You didn't report him to the police."

She shook her head. "It was only twenty dollars. And yes, I know it probably wasn't the first time he'd taken money, but it might have been, mightn't it? I hated the idea of being responsible for him having a juvenile record."

"Did you tell his parents?" This wasn't quite a question—tinged as it was with resignation, the police chief already knew the answer.

"No."

His mouth twisted. "Well, just because he got lucky doesn't mean this kid isn't resentful. This strikes me as something a teenager would do. Impulsive and mean-spirited."

Rory, Charlotte thought, was also impulsive and mean-spirited. She had a suspicion his emotional maturity had stuck somewhere in the mid-teenage years. But she'd said enough last night and didn't want to further upset Faith.

Wheeler glanced at Charlotte. "This Hardesty. Does he live in West Fork?"

Faith had gone back to examining the tablecloth. "Yes."

"Anyone else you can think of?"

Both sisters shook their heads. Charlotte wasn't entirely sure Faith would have noticed if someone hated her with a passion.

"All right." Chief Wheeler closed the notebook and pocketed it, swallowed the last of his coffee and pushed back the chair. "I'll be talking to neighbors in case anyone saw anything, and to

Hardesty and Coffey both. I'll let you know what I learn."

Faith and Charlotte both rose to their feet, too. There was something rather intimidating about Ben Wheeler when he towered over them.

Faith looked flustered, and Charlotte remembered her sister hadn't yet had breakfast. "It's almost ten," she said. "I'll walk Chief Wheeler out and open up shop. You need something to eat."

"Thank you." Faith sounded genuinely grateful. "I'll hurry."

After assuring her sister that she could manage for half an hour, Charlotte allowed Chief Wheeler to open the back door for her.

The day was already too hot, as far as she was concerned. She had begun to miss the fogs that rolled in from the Pacific Ocean on hot San Francisco days.

As they walked toward the barn, Charlotte said, "So what did we do to deserve the police chief's personal attention?"

He appeared to be amused. "Gray called me. He considered your fire a priority."

Oh.

After a moment, Charlotte said, "Faith doesn't want to think Rory is a danger, but he gave me the serious creeps."

"So I gathered." He glanced down at her. "Will you call the next time he shows up?"

"I will. I told him he wasn't welcome on our land. I doubt Faith would call 9-1-1, though, just because he stopped by. She's delusional where he's concerned." Blunt, she thought, but true.

They were nearly to the barn before Wheeler spoke again. "Does she still feel some attachment for him?"

Charlotte frowned. "No, I don't think so. It's just her nature to expect the best of anyone." She made a face. "We may look alike, but that's as far as our resemblance goes."

Some emotion flickered across his face, too quickly for her to read. They had reached the front of the barn and the hard-packed dirt parking lot, where his squad car waited. Charlotte dug the barn key out of her front pocket, since they had locked up earlier when they returned to the kitchen.

Why lock the barn door once the horses have gotten out? she thought irreverently, but of course Faith had been right; they didn't want customers to wander around unattended.

A car was hesitating on the highway right now, the driver apparently drawn by the large hand-painted signs promising, Antiques! Fresh Produce! Plant Nursery! Local Arts & Crafts! Corn

Maze! No, she reminded herself, the sign for the corn maze was covered for now.

Wheeler cleared his throat. "This is a little bit unprofessional… Hell, probably a whole lot unprofessional. But I'm wondering if you'd consider having dinner with me."

Charlotte blinked in surprise and faced him again. She'd have sworn his gaze had lingered more on her sister's face than hers, but who knew? Maybe Faith's obvious shyness or unease or whatever it had been had scared him off. And, hey, they did look alike.

He was a really sexy man.

In a flash, she thought, *If I start dating Ben Wheeler, I'll be safe from Gray.* And Ben was attractive; she could enjoy spending time with him, maybe even kissing him. Couldn't she?

"Sure." She smiled at him. "That sounds like fun. When and where?"

"Why not tonight? There's a pretty good new restaurant right here in town. Not too fancy, but good food, if you like steaks."

"I like steaks."

They agreed on a time, and he left in the usual cloud of dust as the first customers of the day pulled in. Charlotte unlocked the barn, turned on the lights and welcomed the older couple, who advanced uncertainly into the cavernous interior of the barn.

"Plants are outside," she told them. "Let me just open those doors." Seeing them both staring toward the burned side of the barn, she added, "Uh…we had a bit of excitement last night. I apologize for the mess. Probably local teenagers, but we're mad as all get out."

Throwing open the side doors and letting in the sunshine, she mused, *A date. Imagine that,* and refused to let herself wonder what Gray Van Dusen had been about to say to her, right before Faith and Ben Wheeler had interrupted them.

"DAD THINKS THEY'LL LET HIM come home on Monday, but he's still going to be bedridden for a couple of weeks," Charlotte said, while she used the steak knife to cut a bite of filet mignon.

"Are you two going to be able to take care of him and run the business, too?" Ben Wheeler asked.

They were in a booth at the River Fork Steakhouse, their dinners in front of them. They had already gotten the getting-to-know-each-other stuff out of the way. She'd learned that he had grown up in Los Angeles and been a lieutenant with the LAPD when he decided he'd like a different lifestyle and had looked around for a small town that needed an experienced cop to head its police department.

"It's a change," he said, not sounding so sure the change was a good one. "I didn't expect the politics."

"Politics?" she asked, surprised.

"The city council. Some days, our esteemed councilors make me wish for a good old-fashioned liquor-store holdup."

Charlotte had laughed, but he'd looked as if he almost meant it. Small town policing must be considerably more aggravating than it had looked from afar.

After hearing about what she did for a living and sympathizing about the layoff, he'd asked about her father and their plans for the farm.

"Faith has thrown herself into this heart and soul," she said. "But she's a teacher, too. Kindergarten. In just a few weeks, she'll be getting her classroom ready. I haven't started looking for a job yet, but I can't imagine staying past September, say. I don't want to run an antique store slash produce market slash corn maze."

It was a cry from her heart. Helping out for a few weeks, sure, but she couldn't imagine what made Faith want to do this long-term. And Dad, laconic at the best of times, was not a man made for retail work. But if they hired too much help, they'd pare their small profit down to nothing.

Faith, Charlotte was very much afraid, had her

finger in a dike that was going to crumble no matter what.

"Well, we'll see," she said with a sigh.

"Could be your sister didn't want to spend too much time thinking after the divorce," the man across the table from her observed. "This was one way of keeping busy."

"I suppose that's possible." Reluctantly she examined the idea. Faith had always clung to the familiar. She'd never considered going far away to college. To her, it had seemed completely natural, after graduating, to apply for a teaching job in her hometown, and marry a boy she'd known since high school. That was the life she'd always wanted. But then Mom died, Faith had to give up on her marriage, and Dad started talking about selling the farm. Too much change.

She couldn't save Mom or her marriage, but the farm was different. So she'd focused all her desperate need for a predictable life on this long shot. God knows, Charlotte admitted to herself, Faith had melded creativity and hard work to succeed to an astonishing extent. Just…not enough. Especially given that business was sure to become something between slow and nonexistent come winter.

She reminded herself that somehow, Dad and Faith had eked through the last year.

Uh-huh. On Faith's paychecks from the school district.

"You haven't mentioned the fire," Charlotte said, changing the subject. "Did you learn anything today?"

"None of the neighbors saw a thing."

"I'm not surprised."

"No," he agreed, and took a bite before adding, "I talked to Hardesty. He gave me an earful about you. Said of course you'd blame him."

"Jerk," she muttered.

"Insisted he loves Faith and knows how important the farm is to her."

Charlotte scoffed under her breath.

"Yeah, that could be taken one of two ways, couldn't it?" Ben remarked. "I'll tell you, though, my gut feeling was that he didn't do it."

Every instinct Charlotte had disagreed, but it was true that she was biased. "So now what?" she asked.

"I couldn't track Coffey down today. His mom says he'll be home tomorrow."

Charlotte nodded.

"Your sister ever considered getting a big dog?"

"We had a dog when I was growing up, but the highway is a worry, and what good would a dog do if he was kenneled or in the house at night?"

"Dogs bark. You'd have an early warning system."

"That's true." She thought about it for a moment before agreeing, "I'll suggest it to Faith. She's always loved animals."

"Just don't let her bring home a cute puppy. You need a dog with some teeth right now."

He must share some of her unease, Charlotte thought, or they'd be talking about something else. Like their favorite music or how they felt about people who used the express checkout in the grocery store even though they had too many items. Whether they were morning people or night owls. The little stuff that mattered, when a man and woman were drawn enough to each other.

"Was it Gray who hired you?" she heard herself ask, and cringed inwardly.

Ben didn't look surprised at her question. "I guess you could say so, although I had the impression the city council had a pretty strong voice."

"So you must be doing okay at politicking," she pointed out.

He sawed at his steak with unnecessary force. "They didn't hate me then. You're right about that. Their enthusiasm for me started to wane when I told them know how grossly understaffed and underequipped their police department was.

Asking them to open the checkbook was the equivalent of giving a woman a poison ivy bouquet on the first date."

Charlotte laughed. The smile was still lingering on her mouth when her gaze was drawn to a man walking into the restaurant. Gray, wearing the suit from earlier, although he'd now added the coat.

He was scanning the restaurant as he walked in, just as she'd noticed Ben doing. Ben was probably assessing diners for their likelihood of turning violent, though, while Gray presumably had voters on his mind. No matter what he was thinking, what it meant was that he saw her as quickly as she saw him. His stride checked as he looked at her, then at Ben, who was turning his head to see what had caught her attention.

Charlotte's stomach knotted at the expression on Gray's face. Shock, followed by… She wasn't sure. Anger? Hurt? Something that darkened his eyes and made a muscle jump on his jaw.

Someone called his name, and he very deliberately turned away to greet a couple at one of the tables with an easy smile. Charlotte looked away from him to find that Ben was contemplating her. He didn't say anything, though, for which she was grateful.

She asked him about juvenile crime in West

Fork and whether drugs were getting to be a problem here, but didn't hear his answer. She was too conscious of Gray, making his way around the restaurant, pausing at almost every table to shake hands and exchange a few words with people. She couldn't seem to make herself take a bite. She felt sick and guilty, and mad because there wasn't any reason in the world for her to feel either. She didn't want to know what her face gave away when he reached their booth.

"Ben. Charlotte." He didn't seem interested in shaking either of their hands.

Humor in his voice, Ben said, "You stop by every Friday and Saturday night just to glad-hand?"

"Actually, I've usually had enough of the good citizens of West Fork by dinner time. No offense," he said politely to Charlotte. "I'm having dinner with Ed Tolman and Don Scheff."

Ben nodded, looking unsurprised.

"City council members?" Charlotte ventured. She'd gone to school with a couple of the Tolman kids. Ed owned the hardware store in town.

"Yeah." Ben smiled at her. "Didn't you see me sink down in the booth when they came in?"

Why didn't a smile that wicked make her heart go pitty-pat? *Because I'm an idiot,* she mourned.

Gray's eyes rested on her face, but she didn't have the courage to meet them. After a moment he lightly rapped his knuckles on the table, said, "Have a good dinner," and left them. Out of the corner of her eye, she saw him join two older men in a booth that was close enough for her to hear the murmur of their voices but not what they said.

Charlotte tried for all she was worth not to be lousy company, but despite her best efforts she kept catching herself straining to hear Gray's voice, picturing his face, wondering what he was thinking.

She hated responding so strongly to a man. She never had before. Faith used to tease her about being commitment phobic, which might have been true back then. No guy, she had always told herself fiercely, was keeping her in West Fork. But even later… Maybe she shied away whenever a man got too serious, or maybe she just hadn't met the right one.

All she knew was, she'd been desperate to escape her hometown, while Gray Van Dusen had chosen to make West Fork his life. She wasn't going to be idiot enough to let herself be tempted by him.

Which meant it was a good thing he'd seen her tonight having dinner with Ben Wheeler. That had been her plan, hadn't it? She bet he wouldn't be stopping by the Russell farm again anytime soon.

She just wished she could forget the look of hurt on his face that he hadn't been able to hide quite fast enough when he first saw her with Ben.

CHAPTER FOUR

FAITH WAS ASHAMED OF HERSELF to be so glad when Charlotte offered to grocery shop and departed, list in hand. In all the years of conflicted emotions toward her twin, she'd never been jealous before. Last night, she was.

There wasn't any good reason for it. Ben Wheeler had asked Charlotte out, not her; it was Charlotte who drew him, not her. And Char had no idea Faith had wished it was otherwise.

And wasn't that pathetic? She was twenty-nine years old, and she'd never in her life felt that twist of desire when setting her eyes on a man. The sight of a smile had never had her heart flopping in her chest like a trout hooked and tossed to shore. Faith had had boyfriends in high school, and then Rory, but her relationship with Rory had been a gradual settling into a contented belief that he was a man she could be happy with, a man who wanted the same kind of life she did. It hadn't been like walking into a glass door, leaving her dazed but still able to see through to where she'd meant to go.

Last night, she'd sat in the living room pretending to read while Char and Ben stayed outside in his SUV and talked or made out for a good fifteen minutes. By the time Char came in the kitchen door and the SUV turned in a circle and left, Faith had stiffly stood in one position so long her body felt locked. She'd thought she might crack when she had to turn her head to greet her sister.

It *hurt,* damn it. She knew it wasn't Char's fault that Ben wanted her instead, but Faith figured she was entitled to a sulk anyway, and that's what she was indulging in.

Her brooding made this a lousy time for her to look out of the barn and see a squad car pull in and West Fork Police Chief Ben Wheeler get out. If Char had been here, Faith knew damn well she would have bolted for the house.

Instead, as she watched him saunter toward the counter, his narrowed gaze first scanning the barn and finally settling on her, she summoned an unruffled smile and said, "Chief Wheeler. I didn't expect to see you today."

He raised his brows. "I told you I'd let you know what Coffey and Hardesty had to say."

"Char told me you don't think Rory set the fire."

He leaned against the counter. "If he did, he's a good liar."

"He can be," she said with more restraint than she felt. She didn't like remembering how, after hitting her, Rory would take her to the hospital and hover with such love and worry on his face, not a single doctor or nurse had ever questioned her broken bones or vicious purple bruises.

"I'm a little less satisfied today," the chief said. "I sat down with Sean Coffey an hour ago, and I'd have to say I agree with your assessment of him. He flushed a little when he insisted that the time you caught him was the first time he tried to steal from you, which tells me it wasn't. But temptation overcame him because he wanted something real bad, and I think he was telling the truth when he said he was grateful you hadn't called the police or his parents."

"What did he want so bad?" she asked.

"Does it matter? Stealing wouldn't have been a solution even if he'd been trying to pay for his sister's chemotherapy."

Faith let out a gasp. "Laurel has cancer?"

The amusement crinkling his dark eyes made her mouth go dry. "No, I was giving a for-example. I don't even know if the boy has a sister."

She felt like an idiot, but stammered, "He does. But that was silly of me."

The amusement died, leaving something disturbing on his face. He quickly masked whatever he'd been thinking. "Not silly. I forget that everyone in this town knows everyone else, and cares. I'm sorry, Faith."

"No, it's okay." She exhaled, hoping he didn't notice how ragged such a simple thing as breathing had become for her. "So where does this leave us?"

He straightened away from the counter and moved his shoulders in a way she took for frustration. "Nowhere, unfortunately. My best guess is still teenagers, but we may never know unless our firebug has a big mouth and talks to the wrong person."

"Or comes back," she said softly.

His eyes seemed to darken. "Or comes back."

"Well." Faith gave herself a shake. "I appreciate you trying. That's all I can ask." She was good at smiling even when she was in turmoil, so that's what she did now. "I hope you and Char had fun last night."

"Your sister is a nice woman."

"Yes, she is."

Over the top of her automatic agreement, he said pensively, "Neither of us went out with each other for the right reason."

"What…what do you mean?"

"We were both thinking about someone else."

"Char?" Faith in astonishment. "She told me

she isn't dating anyone else. Are you saying she's nursing a broken heart?"

Was it possible? Char?

"I think she's got her eye elsewhere and doesn't want it to be." He shrugged. "And I shouldn't have said that. She'll tell you when she's ready."

"We're…" Her throat clogged. "We're not close."

"That's not the impression I got."

Her temper flared, and Faith snapped, "Then you were wrong." She sighed. "I seem to be in a mood. I'm sorry."

"You don't have to be." His voice, rough enough to sound damaged, had inexplicably become gentle. "Faith…"

She wanted to ask who *he* had been thinking about when he asked Char out, but of course she couldn't. The way he was looking at her right now made her heart pound, which churned up panic. "What did Rory say about me?"

Whatever she'd imagined she saw was gone, just like that. His expression was no more than courteous. "He said he respects you and wishes he hadn't blown it. Said he's mad at himself, not you. I suggested the best thing he could do for you is stay away, and he agreed."

"I wish he would. That's not too much to ask, is it?" She hated how pathetic she sounded, but couldn't help herself. Just thinking about Rory made this awful pressure build up in her chest until she could hardly bear it.

"Charlotte is right," Ben told her. "You call me if Hardesty steps foot on this property."

Her head bobbed without any conscious volition. "Yes. Okay. You're both right. I'm a wimp."

"I didn't say that."

"You didn't have to." God knew how, but she smiled again. "Thank you again, Chief Wheeler."

He hesitated, looking like he might like to say something else, then responded, "Good day, Ms. Russell," and left.

She hadn't been able to repress a tiny flicker of excitement when he'd said, "We were both thinking about someone else," but it died now, as if she'd dumped a bucket of water on it.

Why, she asked herself, *would a man like him have any interest at all in a woman who'd been so weak she'd allowed herself to be battered?*

GRAY COULD HAVE TAKEN A different route between city hall and Van Dusen & Cullen, Architects, but most often he drove down Main Street despite the stop signs at every corner. He liked the fact that there wasn't a single chain store downtown. They wouldn't have looked at home in this classic small town with false-fronted stores, apartments above the street-level businesses and flower baskets hanging on lampposts.

When he'd sat on the city council and since he had won the mayoral election, he'd had a part in keeping every building tenanted and in bringing the chain stores inside the city limits, but keeping them out by the freeway. He wanted their tax money and he wanted their conveniences for the citizens of West Fork, but he wanted to hold on to the character of a town that had survived a century without taking on any big-city problems.

Some of those were pressing now, but he intended to do his best to head them off. At the upcoming city council meeting, for example, he and Ben Wheeler would ask for the funding to put a police officer half-time in the schools. *Before* drugs and gangs crept inside the city limits.

He'd chosen West Fork for reasons he knew were intensely personal. He couldn't recapture a time when his family was happy, before he'd lost his brother and, in a way, his parents, too, but that was the kind of life he longed for and fully intended to build. He hadn't started a family of his own yet, which had left him free to concentrate on shaping this town to his liking.

That was arrogant, maybe, but he believed that most people shared the same desire for a hometown that was safe, where people knew and watched out for each other, where big-city conveniences were available, but not so nearby that giant parking lots replaced quiet streets where neighborhood kids could ride their bikes. He was helping make that happen. For his own reasons, granted, but Gray liked to think he was simply more aware of what drove him than most people were.

He glanced at Tastee's in passing, thinking about the little white caps and how the candy-striped shirt would have looked on a teenaged Charlotte Russell. That's when he noticed the battered pickup parked right in front. He pulled into a parking spot half a block farther down the street before he had time to reason himself out of it.

Charlotte might not even be the one inside. Faith could have taken the truck to town. And he wasn't altogether sure he wanted to see Charlotte anyway. He'd half expected to wake up this morning with a huge, ugly bruise on his chest from the blow he'd felt last night at the sight of her sitting across the table from Wheeler. He would have sworn she shared the attraction, the pull that was more than physical.

It seemed he was wrong. So what the hell was he doing, pushing open the door and entering Tastee's because Charlotte might be there?

He'd have an ice-cream cone. That was all.

But Gray had already spotted her, sitting alone

at a table with a sundae in front of her. As he watched, she lifted a spoonful of ice cream to her mouth and savored it. Her tongue came out and slid over her lips, searching for more flavor.

She didn't mean to be sexy, but his knees damn near buckled.

He had to wrench himself away to turn and order a scoop of French vanilla ice cream. But when he turned back, cone in hand, she still hadn't noticed him and remained focused on her sundae. Not until he pulled out the chair and sat across from her did she look up with that familiar flare of wariness in her blue eyes.

"We keep running in to each other," she said, after a moment.

"It's a small town." He took a bite of ice cream.

"Doesn't that make your teeth hurt?"

He swallowed, ran his tongue over his teeth and smiled. "Nope. What do you do, lick a millimeter off at a time?"

"*I* use a spoon." She brandished the pink plastic utensil.

"Spoons are for old ladies. You should try to have some fun."

Sounding smug, Charlotte said, "It's fun when hot fudge is involved."

He'd never been aroused so fast, not even by a striptease. All it took, apparently, was a too-thin, nervy woman who took her slow, sweet time enjoying her ice cream.

He wondered how many of her subtle curves Ben Wheeler had laid his hands on last night.

"And what's that you're eating?" she asked. "Vanilla? Gee, why don't you try to live a little?"

"I'm a simple man. I like my pleasures uncomplicated." *Sometimes,* he thought. Charlotte Russell seemed as complicated as a woman could be.

She took another bite and murmured with pleasure.

"Sounds like Wheeler has reached a dead end," Gray said in a voice that was only a little scratchier than it should have been.

"Oh?" Charlotte poked the spoon in the sundae and looked at him. "Have you talked to him since he went to see Sean Coffey?"

"Yes, and he can't see the kid having done something so vicious."

Her expression hardened. "Vicious sounds a whole lot more like Rory Hardesty."

"You called him a wife beater."

Her fury glittered in her eyes. "He hurt Faith. And she lied to us, her family. She always had an excuse for the broken bones or the black eye, for the days she had to take off work because she was 'sick.' My parents didn't see through the lies.

If I'd been here—" It was as if a knife had sliced her sentence off, between one word and the next. She squeezed her eyes shut, then opened them to look at Gray. "But I wasn't," she finished, the very flatness of her admission telling him how much she hated making it.

"If she wouldn't tell your parents, what makes you think she'd have told you any more?"

"We read each other well." She paused. "That's one of the tribulations of being a twin."

Gray remembered what it was like having someone who knew what he was thinking as soon as it crossed his mind. He'd never gotten over losing his brother, never would. But he hadn't talked about Gerrit with anyone but his parents in over fifteen years, and rarely even them. Thinking about Gerrit, remembering, hurt them. The absence of his brother and their inability to talk about him was the shadow that kept him from feeling as close to his parents as he'd like to have been. They loved him and he loved them, but he always wondered if his every visit peeled scabs from unhealed wounds.

Not a comfortable thought.

Bothered by his lapse into old regrets, he only nodded at Charlotte's observation, although the words *I had a twin* crowded his tongue. He might have told Charlotte, if he hadn't seen her last night with Wheeler.

"Well, it's over," she said with a sigh. "Or it would be, if Rory would get it through his head that so far as Faith's concerned, he's history." She narrowed her eyes at Gray. "I suppose you're going to tell me some teenager set that fire just for fun, too."

"No. I'm with you. I heard how that bastard talked to you. You pissed him off royally. When he left that day, he was mad. I think that fire is just his style."

She blinked. "Well."

He gave a slow smile. "Surprised you?"

"Wheeler ticks me off," she muttered. "Why can't he see through Rory? Are you sure he knows what he's doing?"

Well. Gray didn't say it aloud, but thought it. He supposed he just stared for a too-long moment. "That why you went out to dinner with him? To knock some sense into his head?"

Pink blossomed on her cheeks, yet another surprise. Charlotte wasn't as confident as she wanted the world to believe.

"It's none of your business why I went out with him," she mumbled, then quickly lifted a sloppy spoonful of ice cream to her mouth. Fudge dripped down her T-shirt and she swiped a napkin at herself irritably. "Doesn't that figure?" she grumbled. "But who cares what I look like anyway?"

I do, Gray thought, and wished like hell he didn't. He wasn't about to tell her she was beautiful even when she was messy and bad-tempered.

He said abruptly, "If it was Rory, he's going to be disappointed the fire didn't do more damage. Didn't even keep you from opening the next morning."

There wasn't any color left in her face now. "I know."

"I wish you had someone else with you there at night."

"We're bringing Dad home tomorrow."

"That won't be much help." Frustration and anger close to the surface, he stood to toss his crumpled napkin in the trash can. "You need someone standing watch."

She tilted her head to look up at him. "Ben suggested we get a dog."

Wheeler again. But the idea had merit.

"The county shelter has plenty of them that need homes."

"Yes, but…" Worry darkened her eyes.

"'But'?" he prodded.

"I don't see how Dad and Faith can keep the farm going. What if they end up having to move into a house with a small yard in town? The last thing they'll need is a big dog."

"Yeah." He sat back down. "You're right. And

it wouldn't be in Faith's nature to take the dog back to the shelter."

"No. And she's so weighted down with responsibilities now."

What about you? he wanted to ask. *Why aren't you a happier woman, Charlotte Russell?*

Gray only nodded again and said nothing.

After a minute, Charlotte sighed. "I need to get on to the grocery store. It's just that I remembered how good the ice cream was here."

"I stop once a week or so myself." Which was an out-and-out lie; occasionally was more accurate.

She smiled at him. "I had some serious muscles when I worked here. Let me tell you, on a Saturday evening when you're digging scoops out, one after the other, the forearms get a workout."

"Write it up for a fitness magazine," he suggested, standing when she did and waiting while she dumped the remains of her sundae and the wadded napkins. "Here's a title—The Sweet Way to Arm Definition."

A grin was his reward. "For most people, scooping ice cream is a faster route to a big butt."

He laughed as he held open the door for her. When she stopped beside the pickup, he paused with his hands in his pockets.

"You off to play mayor?" she asked.

"Architect. Did mayor this morning."

"Who is Cullen?"

Pleased by her interest, Gray said, "Moira. Friend of mine from college. She's carrying the firm right now, but she claims not to mind."

Charlotte nodded, although from the speculation in her eyes he guessed she'd have liked to know more. That gratified him, too. Let her imagine what kind of relationship he and Moira had.

Assuming she bothered, of course. Mild curiosity wouldn't torment her the way he'd been tormented last night when he lay awake picturing Wheeler kissing her or—worse yet—wondering if Charlotte had gone home with him.

Irritation with himself made his nod brusque. "See you, Charlotte."

"Sure." She flipped a hand and started around the back of the pickup.

Gray didn't wait to watch her get in. He walked away, his irritation as uncomfortable as a poison-ivy rash, and just as avoidable.

He should have driven on, not stopped for the damn ice-cream cone he hadn't even wanted.

Next time, he told himself, he would drive on.

DON RUSSELL CAME HOME IN an ambulance the next day. From Faith's air of worry, Charlotte guessed that the insurance wasn't covering the extra cost, but her sister had been so edgy that day, she didn't like to ask.

They'd rented a hospital bed and set it up in the living room where he could see both the TV and out the front window. He wouldn't be able to handle stairs for a good long while. He wouldn't be putting weight on his left leg for weeks, either, although he was encouraged to haul himself around some on his crutches.

He looked gray by the time the ambulance workers got him settled in bed.

"I should have gone to a nursing home," he muttered. "This is too much for you girls. Waiting on me hand and foot… A bedpan…" He shook his head.

Faith kissed his cheek. "We're not girls anymore and haven't been for a long time. And what's so different about emptying a bedpan from mucking a stall?"

He glared at her. "A man should be able to hold on to some dignity."

"Nowadays," she told him, "a man has to be able to buy dignity. We can't afford it."

Who'd have thought Faith was capable of being so blunt? Charlotte stepped forward on her father's other side. "I came home to help take care of you, Daddy, and I don't mind. I'm guessing you changed a few of our diapers. Think of it as payback time."

He grumbled some more, but the reminder seemed to mollify him.

The sisters left him to nap and returned to the barn. He had the phone within reach and they both carried cell phones.

"We need to check him at least every hour anyway," Charlotte said as they walked across the lawn. "He'll refuse to call unless he's facedown on the floor, and then he won't be able to reach the phone."

"Maybe every half hour, at least this first day or two," Faith agreed. "Have I thanked you for being here?"

"Only a thousand times or so."

A couple of cars were parked outside the barn and another was turning in from the freeway.

"I think we should open the maze this weekend," Faith said.

"Looks like the corn is tall enough," Charlotte agreed. "I assume that's what you were waiting for?"

"Yeah, it's no fun if you can see over the top."

"You know, I've never been through a corn maze. I guess I'll have to try it out before we open."

Faith grinned at her. "You need to memorize it so you can go on rescue missions."

Charlotte stopped. "You're kidding. Anyone lost enough could just push through the corn."

"But they don't think of that. Kids especially. And I designed a really good maze this year." She started to walk again, then stopped. "Maybe Ben would like to try it with you."

"Wheeler?" Charlotte snorted. "He'd probably like it better if I could lose some city council members in there. Permanently."

They fell into step again. "He having trouble with them?"

"If memory serves me, what he said is that he'd rather have a good old-fashioned liquor store holdup than attend the next council meeting. Or words to that effect."

They were almost to the barn. "Did you like him?" Faith asked.

Charlotte shrugged. "Yeah, he seems like a good guy. Although, still waters, you know?"

Right outside the open doors, Faith stopped again. "Run deep? What do you mean?"

"Just that I wonder why he made such a drastic change in his life. LAPD to West Fork? Not a natural progression."

"No, I suppose not. Did you ask?"

"Yes, but he wasn't very expansive. I could tell he didn't want to talk about it, so we moved on." She shrugged. "You're more likely to get to know him well than I am."

"He asked you out. Not me."

"I think..." Charlotte didn't finish. If Faith hadn't noticed the way he watched her, that meant she wasn't interested, or he scared her, or who knew. Maybe she was off men, after Rory. Who could blame her? Charlotte didn't want to make her sister uncomfortable with the police chief, not when she was likely to need him. The fire wouldn't satisfy Rory for long.

Faith looked hard at her. "What do you think?"

"We didn't have any spark." Charlotte made a face. "Bad pun, huh?"

"He's a sexy man."

Charlotte raised her brows.

Her sister flushed. "I'd have thought he was your type, that's all."

Interesting. "Well, it turns out he's not." She frowned. "Why is it we've never been attracted to the same men? Isn't it supposed to be chemical? We should have the same chemicals."

Despite all her worries, Faith had never looked prettier than she did right now, laughing helplessly as she leaned against the weathered barn, the sun making her blond hair gleam.

"Remember Derek Hinchy?" She could barely

get the words out between giggles. "That crush you had on him?"

"Oh, God." Charlotte found herself laughing, too. "What was that, seventh grade?"

"Yes, and you walked to the library every day after school instead of taking the bus home because he went there."

"And the minute he got there he'd log on to the computer and never look up again."

"I can still picture that lank hair hanging over his face."

"I figured he was brilliant and really deep. But one day he'd see me and…"

"You'd suggest he wash his hair?"

They both went off into gales of laughter again.

"Still," Charlotte said, when she recovered, "my point's valid. I don't remember us ever being interested in the same guy."

Faith opened her mouth, visibly thought better of whatever she'd been going to say, then closed it. It was a moment before she suggested, "I guess we disprove the whole theory. Because think about it—if we give off identical pheromones, the same guys should want both of us."

"Never happened. You're right. We've made a scientific breakthrough."

"And we won't get credit for it." Shaking her head, Faith went on into the barn.

Smiling, Charlotte followed. Derek Hinchy. The first of her geek crushes, and the least excusable. Faith had been nice enough back then to be sympathetic and to help her think of excuses to loiter in his vicinity. In turn, Charlotte had pretended she understood why Faith thought Saul Epler was the hottest guy in the world even though he was six foot two and so skinny he could have passed for a praying mantis. He wasn't very smart, either, she remembered. But, oh, how she and Faith had whispered and giggled about their first crushes!

Funny, Charlotte thought, *how easy it is to forget the good parts of having a sister.*

CHAPTER FIVE

"YOU'RE GOOD AT RETAIL," Faith told Charlotte. "That table yesterday, and the armoire today. Those will really help the bottom line."

They sat in the dining room, which offered more room to spread out papers than the smaller kitchen table. The TV in the living room was on, but Dad had fallen asleep in the middle of one of his favorite shows. He seemed to be doing that a lot. Charlotte guessed the pain pills were pretty potent. Once he started to snore, she and Faith had retreated, Faith to pay the bills and Charlotte to go through some of their father's files. He'd been too fuzzy to remember the details of their insurance coverage. A talk with the agent had already told them that the retail items lost in the fire weren't covered. Tonight, Charlotte was determined to make sure they knew where they stood otherwise. Thanks to their deductible, they were already bearing most of the cost of replacing the stretch of barn wall that had been burned. The man Gray recommended had started work two days after the fire and planned to finish tomorrow. He'd salvaged old wood from somewhere, so there was no raw wood to stick out like a sore thumb.

She looked up from the homeowner's insurance policy. "The woman who bought the table had made up her mind before I said, 'May I help you?' The couple with the armoire...I guess I did push a little. Scared 'em into thinking it would be gone if they thought about it too long."

"I can never push," Faith said sadly.

"Oh, bull!" Charlotte snorted at her sister's startled expression. "You can't tell me you didn't have to push all kinds of people to get the farm business going. Starting with Dad. And you must have gotten business permits, and found connections for the nursery plants and antiques. Not to mention bullying all the artists into paying a commission to have their stuff here!"

"Bullying?"

"And what you said to Dad the other day, about not being able to afford dignity."

"That was mean, and I wished I hadn't said it the minute the words were out of my mouth."

"No, it was blunt. And in this case, true. It's not always bad to be blunt."

Faith's eyes narrowed. "You mean, I should have been blunt with Rory."

"I wasn't thinking about him," Charlotte said, and meant it. "Blunt wouldn't have cut it with

Rory. Too subtle. He needed a knee in the balls. Or to look down the barrel of a shotgun."

Faith blinked. "Too subtle?" Then she cracked up.

Okay, that was a surprise. Charlotte had been afraid she'd offended her sister again. But it seemed like she'd been loosening up the last couple of days. *Or maybe I've been loosening up,* Charlotte thought. Spending time with Faith, talking to her—really talking to her, not just making conversation—had been easier than she'd expected. And…nice.

The phone rang, and Faith sprang up. "Damn it, that'll wake Dad!"

She made it to the kitchen phone before the third ring, but came back to the dining room almost immediately. "Nobody there."

They looked at each other uneasily. Dad had complained earlier of at least two hang-ups.

"Did you hear anything?" Charlotte asked.

"No. Whoever it was hung up right away. No heavy breathing, no giggling in the background. It probably was just a wrong number."

"Isn't there some way we can check the caller's phone number?"

Faith frowned. "Yes, but I don't remember. I suppose it's in the phone book."

"No, that's silly. Unless we keep getting these."

For a woman living alone—as Faith had been until Charlotte came home—phone calls like that could be scary. But with three adults in the house, hang-ups were more pathetic and annoying than anything.

Faith nodded. They worked in semisilence for half an hour, Charlotte occasionally sharing some tidbit she unearthed, like the fact that Dad didn't have flood insurance, which could be bad in the event of a hundred-year flood.

"The house is built up high enough," she said, "but the barn isn't. Dad used to just get the cows to high ground if the water was rising, but moving everything in the barn wouldn't be that easy. You might want to think about adding the extra coverage before winter."

Faith rubbed her forehead. "I don't know if I can afford to add anything."

"Once I have a job again, maybe I can help some."

Faith offered a twisted smile. "No, if we can't become self-sustaining, we'll have to give up. I can keep working this hard if we're making it, but not if it's taking every penny of my paycheck from the school district and bailouts from you, too." She shook her head. "No."

Charlotte was about to ask why it was okay for Faith's salary to go to keeping the family farm but not hers, but she was distracted by something outside the window. Movement, or a sound, or…? She turned her head, puzzled.

The window imploded and something smashed onto the table, then rolled to drop on the floor. A rock that had to be eight or ten inches across, Charlotte realized as she leaped to her feet. Faith was doing the same, but because she'd been closer to the window she was shaking off shards of glass and—oh, God—had blood streaking her cheek and dripping from a cut on her upper arm.

In the living room Dad was bellowing.

"Don't try to get up!" Charlotte yelled, starting around the table to her sister.

She saw another flash of movement outside, in the dark. An arm swinging. It lobbed something else through the window, something that had a sparkling tail, like fireworks. Sizzle, sizzle, crackle.

Boom!

The stunning explosion had them both hitting the floor, covering their ears. Too late.

A cherry bomb, she thought. Some son of a bitch had just tossed a cherry bomb through the dining-room window. She scrambled to her feet and raced for the back door.

She couldn't hear anything but ringing in her ears, but she flung open the door and all but fell down the steps, then ran for the side of the house. Damn, it was dark out here. Darker for her, with her eyes adjusted to indoor light. Even so, she saw someone running. Headlights from a passing car on the highway glinted off metal—an SUV or pickup pulled onto the shoulder. She sprinted after the bastard who'd thrown the cherry bomb, but the vehicle was moving long before she reached the highway. Fishtailing on the dirt and gravel, it accelerated onto the highway without lights. She could barely make out the shape of the vehicle, much less the color.

Gasping, she stopped, bent and braced her hands on her knees. As soon as she could fill her lungs with oxygen, she straightened and headed back to the house at a trot.

Faith. She'd been on the floor bleeding when Charlotte had raced out of the kitchen. And she'd been closer to the cherry bomb when it went off.

Dad. Oh, Lord. What if he'd tried to get out of bed and fallen?

She was terrified by the time she stumbled back into the dining room and saw Faith sitting up, her back to the wall. Her face was pale, and she was bleeding from half a dozen cuts that Charlotte could see at a glance. Her terrified gaze lifted to Charlotte.

She said something. Her voice was tinny and far away.

"I couldn't catch him," Charlotte said. "I'm sorry."

She could hardly hear herself, and could tell that her sister had no idea what she'd said.

"Dad?" She went to the living room. He was propped up on his elbows. When he saw her, he dropped the phone onto the bedcovers and held out one arm.

Tears in her eyes, she let him hug her, just for a minute, before she pulled back. "Did you call 9-1-1?"

He nodded and talked. She had to shake her head. "I can't hear you. Faith…Faith was closer. She's okay, but she has cuts from the glass, and…"

The ringing in her ears was getting higher and higher pitched. No, she realized, as she hurried back to the dining room. There was a siren outside, flashing lights. She stopped, squeezed Faith's hands, then went to open the kitchen door.

Ben Wheeler came in so fast, she stumbled back. Urgency in his dark eyes, he asked her something. She shook her head again and touched both her ears.

"Faith?" he yelled. "Your dad?"

She motioned toward the dining room. Two EMTs bounded up the steps and came into the kitchen. She waved them forward, too, then sagged for a minute onto a kitchen chair. She was shaking all over and wasn't sure she could have stood.

I'm scared, she thought. *Scared, and mad. That son of a bitch. It was him. It had to be him.*

The ringing in her ears seemed to be subsiding, and she could hear voices. Faith had to be in much worse shape than she was. *Quit being so spineless,* she told herself, and managed to get to her feet and go back to the dining room.

Ben Wheeler was crouched, one arm wrapped around Faith. Her cheek lay against his chest. The EMTs were cleaning up her cuts, dabbing gently but making her wince with the sting of whatever disinfectant was on that gauze. Dad had made it out of bed and stood in the doorway to the living room, propped up on his crutches. He looked stunned and angry and helpless.

Charlotte went to him and rested her forehead against his chest. One crutch clattered to the floor, and once again his arm wrapped her. She let herself burrow for just a moment, treating herself to the illusion of security her daddy's arms gave her.

She couldn't give herself more than that fleeting moment. She hadn't leaned on anyone in so long, it felt unnatural. Straightening, she smiled at her father. "You need to go back to bed."

He swayed, and she saw how gray his color was.

"Now." She bent to pick up the crutch.

"Van Dusen," he said.

Huh? Did Dad think Gray had something to do with the cherry bomb?

Straightening with the crutch, she realized her father was looking past her. Without much surprise, Charlotte turned to see Gray striding through the dining room. He wore jeans, a faded blue T-shirt and athletic shoes.

He didn't even stop to talk to Ben, sweeping him and Faith with a comprehensive look that made Charlotte cringe. Ben's tender care of Faith made it pretty plain to anyone with eyes that he'd asked out the wrong Russell sister.

Just what she needed to go with the ringing ears, Charlotte thought. A dose of humiliation.

He stopped just short of her, his eyes darkened to charcoal. "You're not hurt." His voice was ragged.

"I… Just my ears." She touched one. "Bells are ringing. Everything else is muffled."

"God," he said with suppressed ferocity. "When I heard this address on the police scanner…"

A shudder traveled down her spine. It hadn't reached the base before Gray took her in his arms. His grip was stronger than her father's, his chest broader. His heart slammed in his chest, where her face was pressed.

He'd been scared for her. Really scared.

And that scared *her.*

She wanted—oh, she was ashamed at how much she wanted!—to stay in his embrace. To let him hold her forever. But the strength of that need had her pushing away, almost frantically.

"Dad. I need to get Dad back to bed."

Her father had been watching her and Gray. "I'm going," he said.

Gray gave her arm a squeeze and smiled at her father. "Let me give you a hand, Mr. Russell."

"Goddamn poor timing for me to be laid up," her father muttered. Or said. She didn't know, since she was partially hearing, partially lip-reading. Dad clumped into the living room, laboriously turned himself, then leaned against the bed as he propped the crutches up within reach.

He braced a hand on Gray's shoulder and let the younger man half lift him onto the bed and help him stretch out. He was breathing hard by then and he closed his eyes. "Give me a minute."

Gray turned to Charlotte. "What happened?"

She told him. He scowled when she got to the part about her running outside to try to catch the bastard who'd just thrown the rock and the cherry bomb.

"What in hell were you *thinking?* It didn't occur to you that he might hurt you?"

"If it was Rory..."

"How many times did he put your sister in the hospital?" He shook his head as if in disgust, his eyes hot with anger.

She fired back, "If we can't identify him—"

"You intended to do that from the hospital bed?"

"I'm not completely helpless, you know!"

Gray swore and turned his back on her.

Charlotte would have liked to kick something. Maybe him. But she also felt as though her chest were being compressed. She didn't know if it was embarrassment at her own foolishness, because she *had* put herself at risk, or shock at the genuine fear she'd seen on Gray's face.

Her father put a hand out and she took it. She hated the way he watched her so sadly, as though he thought he'd failed her.

"You couldn't have done anything, Daddy," she whispered.

Gray turned back around, his gaze resting for a moment on Charlotte's hand, linked to her father's. Then he met her eyes. "You think you have to take care of this yourself. Don't you expect Wheeler to do anything?"

"I don't think he *can*," she corrected. "The rock is too rough to hold a fingerprint, and the cherry bomb blew itself to smithereens. I saw movement outside the window, but I didn't see the person." She shrugged, trying with nonchalance to hide her deep sense of helplessness. "We didn't learn anything. Anything at all."

"Did this guy leave on foot or in a car?"

"He was parked by the highway. Since he didn't turn on headlights, I can't be sure what he was driving. I think an SUV or pickup. Definitely not a car."

"Then you did learn something." Gray was suddenly closer to her again, his voice gentle. "I shouldn't have yelled at you."

"Did you?"

His mouth twisted. "I don't know. I wanted to."

Her knees felt wobbly. The temptation to lean against Gray again was powerful enough to awaken a flutter of panic in her belly. All the same, he was being nice, and deserved honesty from her.

"I suppose it was stupid to run out there. I wasn't thinking very clearly."

"Turn your head," he said suddenly, sharply.

"What?"

He cupped her cheek with one hand and pushed her face away. Then he swore again, viciously enough to widen her eyes. "You have a shard of glass sticking out of your neck."

"Don't touch it!" She batted at his hand. "You'll cut yourself."

"Have the EMTs even looked at you?" He sounded pissed.

"Not yet. Faith..."

"Come." He all but pushed her into the dining room and said, "Sit."

"Do I get a Milk-Bone?" Charlotte asked, full of sarcasm.

Faith was gone and so was Ben Wheeler. One of the two emergency medical technicians was cleaning up. After a couple of words from Gray, he was instantly at her side.

The shard of glass he extracted from her neck was half an inch long. The deadly point was red with her blood. She blinked at the sight of it lying on the table.

"I didn't even feel that," she whispered.

"You're probably in shock," the medic told her. He was a stocky man with beefy shoulders and thick fingers that still managed to touch her delicately. He was checking her over carefully now, and had already found a couple more bits of glass embedded in her flesh. "How's your hearing?" he asked.

"Coming back, but still strange. Faith? Were her eardrums damaged?"

"Doesn't look like it, but Chief Wheeler took

her to the hospital to get her checked out. We didn't realize you were in the room, too."

Charlotte pointed at her chair. "That's where I was sitting."

The two men looked at the glass littering the table, at the scar in the finish made by the rock that looked obscenely out of place on the faded Oriental rug, and at the charred remnants of the cherry bomb.

Gray made a sound, as if his breath had been punched out of him. Charlotte was careful not to look at his face. She didn't want to know what she'd see there. The EMT grabbed his otoscope and peered into her ear.

He declared her eardrums to be intact and cleaned up her few cuts. "I'd recommend you have a doctor check you out, too. Tomorrow is probably okay, unless your ears start to hurt or your hearing deteriorates."

She nodded. "Thank you."

Gray was frowning at the window. "I wonder if Wheeler called anyone to board that over."

Charlotte had seen some planks in one of the outbuildings. Despite the exhaustion that had taken the place of her intense adrenaline, she said, "I could probably do that."

Gray's frown deepened to a scowl when he looked at her. "Don't be ridiculous. If you have some boards, I'll do it. You need to go to bed."

"No, I need to check on my father…."

"I'll do that." His large hand, suddenly gentle, squeezed her shoulder. "I'm staying. I'll sleep on the sofa."

"Oh." Her eyes filled with tears, which should have infuriated her. She never cried. But the idea of being able to collapse in bed without having to lie there, stiff, listening for every little sound, was so seductive it called for tears. She sniffed. "Dad snores."

Gray laughed, deepening the creases in his cheeks. "Who knows? Maybe I do, too."

She shouldn't ask. Asking invited…something. She did it anyway. "Don't you know?"

"No." Voice a notch huskier, he said, "I don't usually do sleepovers." He paused. "What about you?"

"Um…none of your business?"

His grin flashed. "I was asking whether you snored."

"That's none of your business, either." She allowed a small smile. "Okay. I'm going to stand up now." Her body seemed disinclined to obey. "Any minute now."

"I could carry you up the stairs."

"Hell, no." She shot to her feet, although she didn't mind the fact that he was hovering, just in case.

She really was fine, Charlotte decided, just a

little shaky yet. Despite Gray's promise, she went to the living room and found that her father had once again fallen asleep, his mouth sagging open. The snore he emitted was low and rough.

She reached for his nearly empty water glass, only to have Gray take it firmly from her hand. "I'll fill this. You get to bed."

"Faith…"

"If Wheeler doesn't bring her back soon, I'll call him. I'll let you know if she's being admitted."

"Okay," she conceded. She bent over her father and skimmed a kiss on his unshaven jaw, so softly he didn't even stir. "'Night, Daddy," she murmured, then started past Gray.

His hand on her arm stopped her. She went very still, but didn't look up at his face. Instead, she focused on his large hand and his lean, muscular forearm, dusted with golden hair. "Sleep well, Charlotte," he finally said. "Don't worry. At least not tonight."

After a minute, she nodded. "Thank you, Gray. For racing to the rescue. And for staying."

"You're welcome." He let go of her arm. "Where do you keep your broom?"

She startled herself with a bubble of laughter at the prosaic question. "Hall closet."

He followed her to the foot of the stairs. Part

way up, she said, “Good night,” and kept going, not looking back to see if he was still watching.

In her bedroom she changed into flannel boxer shorts and a clean tank top instead of a gown, figuring that she should be decent in case the night held any more excitement. After brushing her teeth, she came out of the bathroom to the sound of voices downstairs. Charlotte went to the landing just as her sister started up. Ben and Gray stood in the hall, looking up. Both, she thought, looked grim.

Faith hurried the last few steps and flung herself into Charlotte’s arms. They hugged and murmured stupid things like, “You’re all right?” and “That was so scary!”

Why was it she and Faith were never so close as when they were traumatized?

As if I don’t know whose fault that *is.*

Faith sniffed. “Dad’s okay?”

“Yeah, snoring away. He’s mad at himself, though, because he can’t do some manly thing like standing outside all night with a shotgun.”

As she’d hoped, Faith laughed. “Lord. My whole head feels as if it’s been stuffed full of rags.”

“But your hearing is coming back.”

“Yeah, although you sound weird.”

“You, too.”

They grinned at each other, their arms still around each other's waists.

"Hey," Charlotte said. "How would you feel about a sleepover?"

Delight lit Faith's eyes. "My room or yours?"

"You have a better bed."

"I do, don't I? *I* got the new mattress and springs." She stuck out her tongue. "So there."

"That *was* eighteen years ago," Charlotte replied. "So they aren't exactly new anymore."

"They're still better than yours," Faith taunted.

"That wouldn't be hard," Charlotte said ruefully. "My bed has this dip in the middle."

"Well, it *was* Grandma Peters's—waste not, want not!"

"God. I'd forgotten."

Faith laughed again and disappeared into the bathroom to brush her teeth.

She reappeared, hair brushed and tidily braided, and they snuggled into bed and turned out the light. Even though they weren't touching, Charlotte could hear her sister breathe.

Into the darkness, she asked, "Do you suppose they're both still standing downstairs?"

"Ben and Gray?" Faith was silent for a moment. "Bristling with manliness, you mean?"

"Mmm-hmm."

"I don't know. Ben said something about staying out in his car until morning."

"Gray's sleeping on the couch."

"Tonight...I don't think it meant anything that Ben..."

"Yeah," Charlotte said. "I think it did."

Faith's hand groped for hers and found it. Squeezed. "I'm sorry, Char. I don't know what happened."

Charlotte smiled in the dark. "There's nothing to be sorry for. I like him, Faith. He'd be good for you."

"He asked you out, not me."

"I think you scare him."

"Why would I?" Faith asked softly.

Their hands were still linked. Charlotte was the one to tighten her grip this time. "I don't know."

"Gray?"

She hadn't confided in anyone in so long, she almost didn't. Anxiety washed through her, and she had a desperate desire to roll over and turn her back to her twin. But she closed her eyes and made herself breathe steadily, in and out. Finally she whispered, "He scares *me*."

Faith didn't move, but Charlotte could feel her staring, as if trying to read her sister's face in the darkness. "Why?" she whispered, at last.

"I don't know," Charlotte said, which was

mostly true. No, she didn't want to become attached to a guy determined to spend his life in West Fork, but there was more to it than that. She just didn't know what that *more* was, why he drew her even as he awakened the most primitive of flight instincts in her.

Or why just the idea of him lying downstairs, stretched out on the lumpy old sofa, determined to protect her, tangled up her insides until she felt terribly vulnerable and yet safer than she had in years, all at the same time.

Eventually, Faith murmured a good-night, and Charlotte did the same. When they fell asleep, their hands were still clasped, and it was Gray's face Charlotte saw.

CHAPTER SIX

FAITH AWAKENED TO SUNSHINE and the realization that she was alone in her bed. She wondered if she'd imagined falling asleep with her sister sprawled beside her, within arm's reach. After Char had moved into her own room when they were kids, they'd had "sleepovers" sometimes, when they'd needed to whisper or muffle excited giggles late into the night. Faith treasured the memory of all those times, when for a few hours Char had given her the closeness she craved.

With a sigh, she got up and dressed, grimacing at the sight of herself in the mirror. Her face and neck looked like a teenage boy's after his first attempt at shaving. Dried blood beaded the smaller puncture wounds; white tape and gauze covered the larger ones. Maybe to avoid scaring customers she should lurk out of sight today and let Char handle the counter. Avoiding the mirror, she brushed her hair and plaited it.

Voices drifted toward her as she started down the stairs and she tensed. Had Ben really stayed the night? But she recognized Dad's voice along with Char's by the time she reached the first floor. She turned toward them and went to the living room.

Char smiled at her from their father's bedside. "Sleep well?"

"Amazingly," she admitted. "You?"

"Yeah, I was out like a light."

"You okay, Dad?" Faith asked softly.

His color was better this morning and his jaw fresh-shaven. A basin of soapy water sat on the hospital table they'd rented along with the bed.

"Be better if those damn pills didn't knock me out." His tone was morose. "Lucky Van Dusen was willing to stay."

"Was he still here when you got up, Char?" Faith asked.

"Yes, just finishing a cup of coffee." Charlotte sounded as if she were commenting on the time the newspaper had been delivered. No biggie seeing him first thing in the morning, she wanted everyone—especially her sister—to believe.

"Brought me a cup, too," Dad said in satisfaction.

"No more disturbances, I take it?"

Char shook her head. "Did you expect one?"

"No, but…"

When she trailed off, her sister made a face. "Me, too."

Their father had been watching them with

shrewd eyes. "That was some dedicated public service last night," he observed.

Char kissed his cheek. "This is a small town, Dad. Apparently we're adding some excitement. Now, what do you want for breakfast?"

Faith could tell he wasn't fooled, but she fled his bedside right on Char's heels.

"Scrambled eggs," Char said. "Um…do we have any bacon?"

"Sure." Faith found it in the fridge as Charlotte took the frying pan from beneath the stove and turned a burner on. "I take it Ben didn't stay," she said, keeping her tone casual.

"Gray said he won the toss. And Ben wanted to track down Sean Coffey and Rory first thing this morning."

Faith nodded, glad to hide her face behind the refrigerator door. She took out the milk, margarine and a carton of eggs. "It was nice of Gray to stay."

Char already had bacon frying. "Last night Dad was so shaken up he took it for granted. This morning, the whole time I was in there he was scrutinizing me with slitty eyes. He's working his way up to demanding to know what the hell is going on and whether Gray *really* stayed on the couch."

Faith laughed. "I'll assure him I never let you out of my sight."

"Yeah, you do that. Right after you're done explaining why our tall, dark and handsome police chief felt compelled to hold you on his lap while the EMTs worked on you."

Oh, Lord. "He *saw?*"

"Yup."

"Damn it," Faith muttered. "It didn't mean anything. He just scooped me up and...I guess I was shaking, so..."

"*I* was shaking." Char's grin was wicked. "He brushed right by me."

Faith felt as if her heart was laid bare. "Do you think...?"

"He's got a thing for you? Of course he does. I told you last night. The question is whether it's reciprocated." Charlotte turned the bacon and then eyed her sister sidelong.

She didn't think she'd have admitted having a stupid crush like this to anyone but Char. Who, she reminded herself, had gone on a date with Ben Wheeler just a couple of days ago. But that didn't seem to matter, not after the way Ben had looked at her last night. So she said, "I guess it is. Or it could be."

"Good." Char gestured with the pancake turner. "Would you grab me a plate and some paper towels? The bacon is done."

While Faith had been standing here doing nothing useful. She hurriedly took out a plate and handed over the roll of paper towels, then started cracking eggs into a big ceramic bowl. By the time Char had drained most of the grease, Faith had added milk, salt and pepper and whisked the mixture smooth.

They let the subject drop, Char tending to the eggs while Faith toasted and buttered bread.

By consensus they ate breakfast in the living room with Dad, Faith sitting on the couch and Charlotte on an easy chair that had been pushed against the wall to accommodate the hospital bed. They balanced their plates on their knees.

"So the police chief was here himself last night?" Dad said, his first hunger apparently satisfied.

Charlotte stole a glance at Faith, then said, "You've met him, haven't you?"

He grunted. "He'd damn well better be out there this morning finding that bastard."

"He's trying," Faith said. "But how can he, when neither of us saw who threw that cherry bomb through the window?"

"Who the hell would it be but Rory?"

Not that long ago, Faith would have protested. Not because she wasn't scared of Rory—she knew a part of her would never let go of the fear. But defending him had become automatic at one time, no matter what he did to her. That wasn't the only reason she hadn't wanted to believe Rory was tormenting her, though. If the arsonist had been a teenager, she wouldn't have had to be as frightened. Even Sean, if he was mad about being fired, wouldn't be relentless. His pique could be satisfied.

But Rory… Rory, she thought, might never be satisfied, short of her crawling back to him on her knees, or dying. That last time he'd beaten her, she'd seen rage so bottomless on his face she had known that might be her last chance to escape him. He was going to kill her, she had no doubt about that. If a neighbor hadn't heard her scream and called 9-1-1, Faith knew she would have died that night.

Neither the barn fire nor the cherry bomb had been intended to kill her, or even hurt her badly. But the two incidents together reminded her of the way he used to work up to the bad beatings. He would do little things to scare her. Sometimes just sneak up behind her, or clean his gun or whet the butcher knife while he watched her. The worst was the time she'd gone up to bed and found a rat lying on her pillow, the head severed from the body.

She'd been a fool to doubt that Rory had set the fire. Now she was convinced. Ben still couldn't do anything, though, not without proof. She knew that after last night, he took the threat seriously. But how could he keep them safe?

The sisters had washed the dishes and gone to open shop when Faith saw the police car pull in. She had been watering in the outside nursery, but turned off the faucet and went in to stand at Char's side. They watched Ben walk toward them, the brightly lit rectangle of the open doorway behind him. Faith blinked, her eyes dazzled.

His gaze went to her first, but his expression was too guarded for her to tell what he was thinking.

"Faith." He nodded. "Charlotte."

Char, of course, simmered with impatience. "Well?" she demanded, even before he'd come to a stop in front of them.

"Last night Coffey was over at Lake Chelan with a friend and the friend's parents."

Faith groped for Char's hand, which closed tightly around hers.

"Hardesty is nowhere to be found. Doesn't appear to have gone home last night. Didn't show up for work or call in this morning."

"Oh, God," Faith whispered.

"We'll find him," Ben promised, his dark eyes steady. "I'm starting with a list of his supposed friends."

She shook her head and it kept shaking like a broken doll's. "He doesn't have any friends."

"I'm told he plays slow-pitch. Has beer after games with some of the guys."

"But they aren't friends. Not the kind who would hide him if he'd done something bad."

Muscles flexed in his jaw. "Some men don't think teaching your wife a lesson is bad."

That momentarily derailed her, because he was right. "Well…I suppose. But when we were married, he didn't have any friends we socialized with. You know? They were all my friends."

She and Rory hadn't socialized with other people at all after the first few months. Her friends had tried to like him, but couldn't. It got to be easier for her to have lunch with them, *sans* husbands. That way no one had to pretend.

"I've got patrol cars watching for his truck. County deputies, too."

"Yes." Now she was nodding, and felt her head bob a couple of extra times. "Okay."

"I called the glass place. They'll be out this morning to replace your window."

"Thank you," Char said.

"Do either of you own a gun?" he asked.

Faith glanced at Char, who after all had become a big-city dweller, but she shook her head. "No," Char said. "Dad has a hunting rifle, but neither of us ever learned to use it. And he'd, well…"

"Take ten minutes to get out of bed and then would be so shaky without crutches he couldn't aim." Ben scowled. "I'd like one or both of you to consider purchasing a handgun and take some lessons to learn how to use it."

"No," Faith said in alarm. "Oh, no. Not me."

Char frowned. "I guess I could think about it, although I've got to tell you, I can't imagine shooting anyone, even a slimeball like Rory."

"Even if he broke in the house?"

Faith was reassured by the way Char shivered. They weren't so different after all.

"I don't know." Char tipped her chin up and met his impatient stare. "I said I'll think about it."

"All right." He frowned impartially at both of them. "Your hearing come back okay?"

They both assured him they were fine.

His eyes lingered on Faith's face, undoubtedly taking in the nicks and cuts. Then he dipped his head, the movement jerky, and said, "I'll be in touch."

Neither sister moved as he strode out.

"Well, so much for clasping me to his bosom," Faith finally said, once his squad car had raised dust outside the barn doors.

"He's definitely running scared." Char was still gazing after him, her expression pensive.

"Let him run," Faith said flatly, turning away. "Rory's giving me plenty to brood about. I'm not going to waste any energy wondering what Chief Wheeler's problem is."

Leaving her sister, she went back outside and turned on the outside faucet.

To hell with Ben Wheeler, she thought, the flash of temper unusual for her, but welcome. It seemed to heat her blood and make her stronger. *To hell with him. No more stupid yearning.*

Fool me once...

With care and utter concentration, Faith went back to watering the potted perennials displayed on long plank tables.

GRAY ATTENDED A COUNTY COUNCIL meeting that dealt with wetlands, zoning and building permits. All of those issues had a significant impact on West Fork, given that much of the recent growth was sprouting just outside the city limits. He had every intention of expanding those boundaries as soon as he could put the pieces for an annexation campaign into place. He didn't think residents of those neighborhoods would protest—he'd heard enough dissatisfaction with response time from the sheriff's department, and folks were frustrated that West Fork residents got cheaper sewer and water rates.

After the meeting, Gray joined half a dozen other mayors of small towns in the north county to confer, grumble, gossip and generally shoot the breeze at a local tavern and steakhouse. He stepped out twice to call Wheeler on his cell phone.

The second time his police chief said, "Damn it, Van Dusen, I've got patrol cars going by every ten or fifteen minutes! What do you want me to do, give them round-the-clock protection? You know how small the force is!"

Gray already knew that Hardesty had yet to turn up. So where was the son of a bitch?

"It's probably too soon for Hardesty to make another move anyway." He leaned against the cinder-block wall of the tavern. Something scrabbled beneath a nearby garbage Dumpster.

"That's my take," Wheeler agreed. "But I plan to loiter at the farm tonight for an hour or so around about midnight just in case."

"Both incidents happened about the same time, didn't they?"

"Yes, they did."

"Huh." Gray rubbed a hand over his jaw, feeling the bristles. "Keep me informed."

"You mean, you aren't going to call me four more times tonight?"

Gray grinned. "Could be. But I'm the boss, right?"

"Oh, yes, sir, you are." On a bark of laughter, his police chief cut the connection.

It was 11:06 p.m. when Gray passed the farm on his way home. The highway was dark and quiet, the lights all out in the house. The moon was but a mere sliver, his headlights cutting a corridor through the night but illuminating only pavement. His foot lifted from the gas momentarily, but he couldn't see a damn thing and if he pulled in he might scare the Russell sisters. He guessed that Wheeler was already there, leaning against the wall of one of the outbuildings or crouched behind an ancient lilac bush.

He went on home, but despite his tiredness had no success in settling to sleep. One o'clock came, two, then three. His phone didn't ring, the police scanner gave away nothing but routine exchanges.

He did drop off eventually, and when his alarm went off he hammered the button with his fist, and groaned when he swung his feet to the floor.

Damn it, damn it, damn it. One way or the other, Charlotte Russell was costing him a lot of sleep.

In the shower he bent his head under the stream and closed his eyes, hands braced. He wondered if Charlotte had slept any better than he had last night. Whether she'd thought about him at all. He remembered the feel of her when he held her, shockingly fragile and yet only able to bring herself to rest against him for a too-fleeting moment. She didn't want to trust him. He doubted she wanted to trust anybody. But him especially, and he knew damn well that was because she'd felt the same punch he had the first time they met, and felt it again every time she saw him.

He suspected he was battering his head against a wall where she was concerned, but he couldn't seem to stop. He might have managed, after seeing her at a candlelit restaurant with Ben Wheeler, had it not been for Hardesty's increasingly nasty assaults on the Russells.

Faith was his prey, not her sister, but Charlotte wouldn't hesitate to throw herself between the SOB and her twin. It was in her combative nature. Charlotte was the one who didn't hesitate to chase after their assailant in the dark with no thought for her own safety, only of her sister's.

Gray wished he understood the tension between the two women. The love they felt for each other was so fierce, it was hard to figure how any other emotion had wedged in there.

He was frowning when he straightened and turned off the shower. He didn't like thinking he and Gerrit would have ever come to be so damn careful around each other. How was estrangement possible, when you had somebody who counted on you as readily as he did his own eyes and ears?

Gray knew what losing that was like, but he'd had no choice. In one fleeting moment of carelessness, Gerrit had been gone—first in a coma, two days later dead. Gray would have traded places with him if he could have, so he of all people understood Charlotte Russell's reckless determination to protect her twin sister.

What he didn't see was any willingness in her to love anyone else, except possibly her father. She sure as hell didn't want to let Gray get close enough to threaten her heart.

So be it, he thought. Chances were she'd end up flying home to San Francisco and not coming back until Christmas, if then. In the meantime, he was going to be there to wrap his arms around her when she needed to lean on someone, even if she couldn't bear to trust him for more than a few seconds. And he'd do anything he could to keep her safe, just as she was fighting to do the same for her sister.

And perhaps, in the meantime, he'd get under her skin. Maybe he could overcome her instinctive wariness. Tempt her.

If he weren't so tired, he'd feel more optimistic.

Telling himself she wasn't what he'd ever imagined wanting didn't help; his sketchy image of an ideal woman had been scrubbed out like the colored charcoal outlines of a drawing on the sidewalk. *She* hadn't been real, she was only the next piece he had to put into place to build the perfect life he'd been so sure he wanted.

Funny, now that he'd met Charlotte—intensely alive, sharply conflicted, bitter and sweet at the same time—he was finding that imagined life no more real than a faded Norman Rockwell print. A kid's dream, not a man's. The man he had become wanted Charlotte, and it was killing him to know that, tempted or not, she was utterly determined to stay away from him.

He spent the morning at city hall returning phone calls, most from citizens who wanted to complain about a neighbor's fence that was surely a few inches taller than the allowed six feet, or the junk car that had been at the curb for a month, or who wondered why their tax dollars were going to pay for fertilizing and daily watering of the huge flower baskets that hung from downtown lampposts, or the addition of some stop signs in residential neighborhoods. He soothed, he offered resources, he promised to look into concerns. He downed ibuprofen and too many cups of coffee.

Instead of taking time for lunch, he went to discuss city ordinances with a resident who kept his half dozen junk cars in his front yard instead of at the curb.

And finally, figuring he could snatch half an hour, he drove out to the Russell farm, just because he wanted to see for himself that one prickly, vulnerable, sexy woman really was all right.

A couple of other cars were already parked in front of the barn. Gray left his Prius beside a Volvo station wagon and walked to the house. He knocked at the back door, then let himself in.

"That you, Char?" Don Russell called from the front room.

"Nope. It's me, Gray." He stepped through the archway between the dining room and living room. "Just wanted to see how you're doing."

The twins' father had the bed cranked up and was, apparently, watching soaps. He lifted the remote and killed the TV.

"You ever try to watch daytime television?"

Gray grinned. "Yeah, I was laid up after a car accident a few years ago. Thank God for DVDs."

Don grunted. "I'd rather read, but these damn pills make it hard to focus on the print."

"If you want, I'll put a movie in for you before I go. Unless—" he nodded toward the now darkened TV "—you'd rather find out what happens to that blonde with the big…"

"Hair?" The older man gave him a sardonic look. "I know what'll happen. She seems to be prone to sobbing. She'll probably fling herself weeping at the doctor who's lying about his divorce."

"Can I get you anything?"

"No, the girls pop in every half hour or so. Seem to think I can't even make it to the goddamn bathroom by myself."

"Can you?"

"Just because I fell once..." He scowled. "This place is too much for my girls. They're working their fingers to the bone while I lie here and watch soap operas."

Gray leaned a shoulder against the woodwork. "You're healing."

Don Russell looked at him with eyes almost as blue as his daughters'. "I don't have the heart for this anymore. I'm a farmer, not a...a... Hell, I don't even know what kind of operation we're running! A minimall! It's not enough to pay the bills, but Faith doesn't want to hear it."

"Charlotte seems to be throwing herself into the business, too."

"For how long?" Don turned his head to stare sightlessly at the front window. The lines on his face were more pronounced than they'd been a minute before, the flesh more sunken. "This isn't the life she wants. It's not the life she should have! Or Faith, either. They deserve better."

Stirred by pity, Gray said quietly, "I think right now it *is* what they both want. They need to know they fought for this place, and for you."

He growled something, then groped for the

button to lower the head of his bed. "If only I weren't so damn muddle-headed..."

"You don't want that DVD?"

"Better shut my eyes again. You go tell the girls not to be poking in here and waking me."

"I'll do that." Gray waited until Don's eyes closed and his mouth went slack, then let himself out of the house through the kitchen.

By the time he reached the barn, one of the cars was gone. He stepped inside, pausing to let his eyes adjust to the dimmer light. Voices came from the nursery area, and he recognized one of them as Faith's. Gray doubted Charlotte knew a penstemon from a phlox. She didn't seem like the puttering-around-a-garden type.

His eyes scanned the barn until he saw her, apparently dusting and rearranging vintage glass and ceramics displayed on a tall, open shelving unit. She didn't notice him until he'd almost reached her, which gave him time to study her.

She was picking up a tan, although her shoulders, bared by a tank top, were peeling. Her skin was too white to surrender to the sun without a fight. Even doing something so mundane, her every movement was tense; she kept moving a set of crystal goblets, as if determined to achieve some perfect placement.

"Hey," he said.

Charlotte spun around fast, the goblet in her

hand brandished like a weapon. "Oh. Gray." Her eyes closed in momentary relief. "You scared me."

"I'm sorry. I just stopped by to make sure I didn't miss some excitement last night."

"Oh, come on." Her self-control restored, she slanted a look at him. "You can't tell me you wouldn't have been kept up-to-date, minute by minute."

He grinned. "Maybe. But I like to see with my own two eyes."

Her brows rose. "That suggests a certain lack of faith in your police chief."

"Not at all. I just like to get out in the community." He nodded at the goblet. "Planning to brain someone with that?"

At last, a smile curved her mouth. "If you'd been that bastard Rory, you'd be face down on the floor this minute." She turned and set it on the shelf, seemingly having lost interest in an artful arrangement. "You're not here because you have news?"

Gray shook his head. "No. Hardesty seems to have gone to ground."

"Unless he just happens to be away, visiting a friend."

"Without calling in to work?"

Her sigh was almost soundless. "It occurred

to me that we could be dancing with the wrong shadow."

"Who else, then?"

"I don't know." She wrapped her arms around herself. "I just don't want to be responsible for us jumping to conclusions."

He had to shove his hands into his pockets to keep from reaching for her, trying to wrap her in his arms. "Do you believe we have?"

"You know I don't," she said, then walked away from him.

Damn it, even now he could help looking at her long legs, at the sheen of sweat on her back above the scoop of the tank top, at her hips just a little too curvaceous to be a boy's. He wanted to touch the back of her neck, where the delicate bones of her vertebrae were exposed. To keep him from making a mistake, he balled his hands into fists in his pockets.

He strolled after her, not surprised when she went behind the counter with the cash register as if to place a blockade between them.

"I see the corn maze is open," he remarked.

She relaxed infinitesimally at the innocuous subject. "Faith says we'll be busy with it this weekend. She claims it's devious enough to bewilder and dazzle the most cynical teenager."

He leaned against the counter, smiling at her. "You tried it out yet?"

"No, and Faith says I have to. Apparently, rescue missions are occasionally required."

Gray laughed. "Someone goes in and doesn't come out?"

"Or you hear a child start sobbing in there somewhere."

His smile faded. "Yeah, that might make you plunge right in." He paused. "Doesn't look like you're too busy right now."

"No. Weekdays seem to be pretty slow." She shrugged, looking unhappy.

Gray nodded. It appeared that Faith was the only member of the family who still entertained hopes that the barn business would succeed.

Right then, Faith came in from the nursery area with another woman who was carrying a cardboard flat of plants. She was apparently taking advantage of the thirty-percent-off sale on perennials that was advertised on a sign out front. The two of them were talking about fertilizer, and Faith grabbed a box of slug bait as she came.

"I'll ring this up," she told Charlotte, who moved aside.

"I thought maybe I'd steal Charlotte and try out your maze," Gray said.

Faith looked up. "Oh, what a good idea! I've been trying to talk Char into walking through it." Strangled sounds came from her sister, but she ignored them and flapped her hands. "Go. Go, both of you!" She flashed a grin. "I'll come hunting for you if you don't reemerge in, say, half an hour."

Gray waited as Charlotte huffed, then snapped, "Oh, fine," and stalked past him as if he wasn't there. Smiling, he followed her. Gray had high hopes that the maze was indeed so convoluted it would take them the entire half hour to find their way out. He wouldn't have a better opportunity to begin his campaign to tempt Charlotte.

CHAPTER SEVEN

"YOU'RE NOT DRESSED FOR THIS, you know." Charlotte knew she sounded irritable and ungracious, but couldn't stop herself. The idea of plunging into the narrow, twisting corridor between tall, thick stalks of corn with Gray Van Dusen breathing down her neck made her edgy, and she couldn't help that.

He'd left his suitcoat and tie in the car. Now he unbuttoned the cuffs of his white shirt and rolled up the sleeves. "Better?"

She snorted. If he wanted to ruin those shiny black wingtips, who was she to argue?

When she looked back at him, it was to find him grinning as he studied the painted plywood arch over the entrance. It was black, with bloodred letters.

Faith had decided it needed a new look this year, and Charlotte had volunteered. The job sounded her style more than some of the farm work. She'd painted it herself, with the help of stencils, and let some of that crimson paint drip like blood, just as she'd painted the arch over the exit, twenty feet to their left. She'd damn near sweated blood, standing on a ladder in the August heat, taping up stencils, painting and clambering down to move the ladder every time the job exceeded her reach. Conscious the whole time she teetered up there of how uneven the rough field was.

All Hope Abandon, Ye Who Enter Here! the letters above the entrance read.

"Dante," he murmured.

"Nice effect, don't you think?"

"Yeah, I do, and it might even educate some of our local heathens."

"Really?"

"No, just wishful thinking." He nodded toward the cornfield beyond the arch. "Lead on."

"Lord." She took a deep breath and started in. "Let's not get lost, okay? Think how embarrassing it would be. And Faith would kill me if I trampled my way out."

"This must have been a hell of a lot of work."

"I think this is the third corn maze she's created. The first year it was just for fun, and open only for a few days before Halloween. Last year she got serious and started charging."

After Faith realized Dad was near to having to sell the farm.

The path curved immediately, so that the

entrance was lost behind them. When it diverged, Charlotte chose the right-hand way at random. The sun, still high in the sky, beat down on them. The corn grew well over Gray's head, and the leaves were thick and green, the cobs swelling in the husks, the emerging silks shimmering gold. The air was closed and still, smelling of turned earth and growing things.

Another Y opened ahead; this time she went left, then a moment later right.

"Dead end," Gray observed, when she faced a wall of corn stalks.

"So I see." She planted her hands on her hips. "You choose next time."

They retraced their steps, and went left, only to be faced immediately with yet another choice. Gray shrugged and went right.

"We grew corn when I was a kid," he said. "A few rows. I never got lost in them."

She liked the picture of him as a little boy, no doubt with a shock of blond hair. Pure mischief, she guessed, except when he was watching people's faces the way he did hers, taking careful note of every nuance of expression.

"Faith and I used to hide in the cornfields," Charlotte heard herself telling him. "We loved knowing no one could find us. We'd whisper secrets and giggle." It was the secretiveness that had held the most appeal; they had a hideout, and no one knew where it was. Not even their parents would have been able to find them. She wondered when Faith had last thought of those times.

"Do you get the feeling we're going in circles?" Gray asked after the path had branched, and branched again.

"Yes." Charlotte stopped and looked around, but how the heck could they tell? One corn plant looked an awful lot like another, and the sun was too high to give direction. "Let's try left again."

"Okay." There were circles of sweat under his arms. It had to be a hundred degrees in here, with no breezes able to find them.

"Maybe we should have water stations."

She loved his stride, long and loose. His body was tall and rangy, lean like a runner's. Charlotte wondered how he maintained his build, hurrying between one job and another the way he did. The only time she'd even seen him out of slacks and dress shoes was when he'd appeared in her house in the middle of the night in those well-worn jeans and a T-shirt that had looked as if he'd snatched it off the floor in his hurry. He'd looked as good in those jeans as he did in his well-cut slacks.

"Mmm." It seemed to be agreement. He stopped so suddenly she almost ran into him. "It's too bad there isn't an easy way to illuminate the maze well enough to have it open on Halloween. Can't you picture jack-o'-lanterns at every Y?"

Ones carved with wicked grins, or with tarantulas instead of faces. Of course, the candles would be too dangerous, but the idea was tantalizing. "We could issue flashlights," she mused.

"Think how many you'd have to buy. And it would be too scary for the younger set. Maybe dangerous for the older kids."

Having a rape happen in their cornfield would not be good PR for the Russell Family Farm business.

"No, you're right," Charlotte said regretfully. "Too bad. It was an idea."

"There might be a way to make it work." His eyes were narrowed as he considered his own vision. "Maybe do it for a charity. Have volunteers dressed as ghosts or what have you placed at regular intervals."

It could be amazing—no pun intended, she realized. Forget haunted houses, their maze would be talked about all year long.

But I won't be here by then.

Charlotte brushed by him and started walking. "Talk to Faith," she advised, over her shoulder, hoping she sounded breezy instead of brusque.

"Maybe I will."

They hit another dead end, and another. He

scuffed an *X* on the ground, then laughed in surprise when they came on it a surprisingly short while later with no awareness they'd made a circle.

"Your sister's good," he said with apparent admiration.

"No kidding." Charlotte pushed her hair back from her face and blinked salty drips out of her eyes.

His hair was darkened by sweat, the brown deepened to bronze, the sun streaks to old gold. As she watched, he undid another button on his shirt and peeled the collar away from his neck. The throat he exposed was tanned. The glimpse of chest and a few curls of light brown hair made her mouth go dry and her knees feel weak.

Charlotte averted her gaze. He could strip and it wouldn't do any good; she was roasting even in the thin tank top and shorts.

"I hope you don't have any meetings this afternoon," she said.

He looked ruefully down at himself. His shoes were covered with dust. The circles of sweat under his arms had spread, and she could have told him his shirt was damp down his back, too, where it was plastered to his spine and to more muscles than she might have guessed he possessed. Dried bits of corn stalk dusted his shoulders and clung in his hair. "I'll go home and change. I am seeing clients this afternoon."

"If we ever get out of here," Charlotte teased.

Damn, he had the most beautiful smile! Relaxed, sexy, warm, just a little crooked. She knew by the humor dancing in Gray's eyes that he enjoyed laughing at himself, not just at others.

"Ten more minutes and your sister is supposed to come looking for us."

"It's been twenty minutes?" Charlotte's back stiffened. "To heck with that!"

"Trust me," he said, "and I'll lead you out."

Her eyes narrowed. "You can see over the top?"

"Occasionally."

"Why didn't you say so?" she asked indignantly.

"And *cheat?*" He was trying hard not to grin, she could tell. "Charlotte, Charlotte. I thought better of you."

She made a sound of such disgust, he gave a shout of laughter. "Ah, Charlotte. I'm going to have to kiss you."

Alarm kicked in, as good as a mule's hoof to the chest. "What?" She backed up, and felt the rustle of leaves behind her.

His laugh was gone, his eyes intent on her face as one long step brought him close enough to crowd her. "You're gutsy about everything but me."

"Maybe I'm just not interested." She was dismayed to hear her voice emerge too high, betraying panic or desperation. "Did you ever think of that?"

"Hmm." His gaze dropped to her mouth. "Why don't we find out?"

She was dizzy, from heat, from the thick air, from the frantic pace of her pulse. Would it be so terrible to find out what it felt like to be kissed by Gray?

Yes. But she'd never yet backed away from an accusation of cowardice, and she wouldn't do it now.

Be honest. You don't want *to back away.*

Waiting, she felt a tremor under her breastbone, an inner quake that was almost enough to make her break and run. Almost. Native stubbornness and, oh, yes, temptation kept her where she was, head tilted back to meet his narrowed gray eyes.

"Good for you," he murmured, in a voice like thick, dark honey. He wrapped one hand around the nape of her neck, fingers tangled in her short dark hair. He bent his head slowly, watching her the entire time.

He must have seen flickers of panic—she wasn't *that* good an actress—but she didn't act on them. At the last second, his gaze lowered to her mouth as if it were a bite to eat. A spoonful of vanilla ice cream, maybe. Her final, foolish thought was, *He must know I'm more complicated than any one flavor.*

And then her eyes drifted shut and his lips brushed hers. Softly. So softly a shiver moved over her, despite the hot, still air. Charlotte didn't move, just waited, suspended in time, until his lips came back to hers.

This time they brushed, then clung. He tugged gently at her lower lip; the tip of his tongue stroked it. Nothing in her life had ever felt as good, and that scared her. Why didn't he just *kiss* her, like most men did? Grind his mouth against hers, stick his tongue in, grope her? Why did he have to be so damn subtle?

His fingers spasmed on her neck; for one fleeting instant, his mouth hardened with intent she understood. But then he lifted his head fractionally, nuzzled her nose with his and said in that husky, thickened voice, "We're running out of time."

Time? For several seconds, she had no idea what he was talking about.

Her knees were all but buckling. Pride kept them stiff. When he let go of her and turned away as if nothing had happened, she might have swayed for a second, but he wouldn't have noticed, because he'd already started down the path to the left.

Charlotte followed dumbly. Indignation was trying to snatch for a foothold in her chest, but it was finding tough going. She felt too much like pudding inside, a fact that should and would infuriate her once she froze up again.

Pudding! she seethed. Did she have to come up with another *sweet* analogy? How about like a sponge? Or pulp, like a pumpkin that had been smashed?

Ahead of her, Gray said casually, "Nope, dead end," and waited while she turned around and went back the way they'd come. A moment later, he turned her left with a hand on her lower back, then right at the next intersection. He was moving with confidence now, even if she wasn't. She clenched her teeth, mad at the realization that he'd gained that confidence at her expense. In fact, he was whistling under his breath, clearly pretty damn pleased with himself. He'd had every intention of kissing her from the moment their eyes first met, she knew he had, and now he'd succeeded.

Yeah, but this kiss was just a preamble. He'd tasted her. *Taunted* her, so that she'd want more.

And, God help her, she did, but if they ever got out of this hateful maze so that a breeze could cool her overheated skin and she could *breathe,* she'd find the resolve to make sure that didn't happen.

"Here we are," he said, a last twist showing them the arched exit only a few feet ahead. Ye Be Saved, it proclaimed.

Charlotte stumbled out. No breeze, but at least the air wasn't so close. "I feel like I should fall to my knees and kiss the ground," she muttered.

Gray laughed. "Come on. It was fun. Admit it."

"Fun?" She leveled an incredulous stare at him. "It was like the outer circles of hell. Quoting Dante was more appropriate than I realized."

He just laughed again, his good cheer apparently not punctured. "Here comes Faith, right on time."

Hand shading her eyes, Charlotte's twin had emerged from the barn. On seeing them, she grinned and waved.

Charlotte flipped a limp hand in return as they started across the field. "Fiend. Now she's going to think I'm qualified for rescue operations, when I have absolutely no idea how we got out of there."

"Remember that most of the day you can use the position of the sun to help some." Gray pulled his shirt away from his chest. "God, I need a shower."

"Me, too." Charlotte felt sticky and disgusting. Gray had probably kept the kiss brief because of her body odor.

Except, she reminded herself, he was sweating every bit as heavily, and she didn't remember noticing any smell except pure male.

"If you want to go on to the house, I'll tell Faith you're taking a quick shower," he suggested.

"Good. Great." Grateful to have her path diverge from his, she cut away immediately.

His voice followed her, quiet and very, very serious. "I'll call, Charlotte."

She didn't answer, just kept walking. But she had to press a hand to her chest, because those inner tremors not only hadn't gone away, they now *hurt*.

DINNER THAT NIGHT WAS a quiet affair. Charlotte was exhausted and Faith was subdued enough to suggest she felt the same. Dad's color was better, Charlotte thought, but every time she looked at him his brow was furrowed and his mouth tight. From pain? Or something else?

"Do you need a pill?" she asked, setting down her empty plate. "I can get you another glass of iced tea."

"I'm all right." He'd only eaten one cob of corn, and this a man who'd been known to have three or four when it was sweet and crisp, just picked from the field like this. But then, Charlotte reminded herself, he wasn't burning very many calories, either, lying in bed all day. Unless enduring pain and frustration counted as an exercise plan.

"Thank goodness they came out so quick to replace the window." Faith set her plate aside, too. "If we'd called, we probably would have had to wait two weeks."

Charlotte was watching and saw the way her father's face tightened at the reminder of the scare.

"Insurance won't cover that window," he said.

After a minute, Faith dipped her head. "The cost was within our deductible."

"What's it going to take, a week's receipts to pay for the damn window?"

Faith flinched.

Charlotte scowled at him. "What are you trying to do, make her feel guilty? Is it supposed to be her fault that Rory's nuts?"

"Don't be ridiculous." He frowned at them both, but some color ran over his cheeks, making her think he felt some chagrin. He pushed the tray table aside, swearing when it lurched after the wheels bumped up against the rug. Faith automatically rose to her feet, but Dad snapped, "Sit down! I'm not completely helpless!"

But he felt helpless, and hated it. His daughters knew it, and he hated just as much seeing the knowledge in their eyes. Charlotte wished she was better at pretence, so she could spare him.

He let out a harsh and unhappy breath. "It's going to be weeks before I'll be any help."

Out of the corner of her eye, Charlotte saw Faith's muscles tighten.

"You're getting better every day...."

"Yeah, three weeks from now I may be able to hobble out to the kitchen and get myself a cup of coffee. It'll be well into the fall before I can get back on a tractor or split wood or give you a break out in the barn."

"We're doing okay," Charlotte said quietly.

His fierce gaze swung to her. "Just how long were you intending to stay? A week? Two weeks? I'll bet you weren't planning on eight, were you?"

No. If she'd had any idea when Faith called that she might be needed that long, Charlotte was horribly afraid she'd have thought of an excuse. But...now that she was here, it was different. It hadn't taken two days here for her to understand that she wouldn't be able to abandon her father and sister anytime in the near future. Just lately, she'd begun to realize that she wasn't here just for them; she was here for herself, too. She'd *needed* to come home. Daddy and Faith's troubles had given her an excuse.

"No, but I don't mind," she said, no longer

shocked because she meant it. "I'd hardly begun applying for jobs and no one has even called me for an interview. You and Faith need me, and I'm glad I can help."

Faith was staring at her, but Charlotte didn't look away from her father's penetrating gaze. It hurt a little to know that he hadn't expected her to be willing to stay, and that maybe he didn't believe she'd stick to what she said.

Would she have, if she'd still hated being here as much as she once had? It made Charlotte ashamed to have to wonder. Maybe part of her need to be home was regaining some lost self-respect.

Dad turned his head against the pillows just enough to pin Faith with that same piercing look. "And you, missy. You're going to have to start getting your classroom ready any day now, aren't you?"

"I have another week or two," Faith mumbled, her mouth sulky.

It was being called *missy* that did it, Charlotte knew. That word, in that tone, was calculated to make either of them feel about eight years old and foolish.

"Uh-huh. And then what? You expecting Charlotte here to take over the whole damn place?"

Faith stole a desperate look at her sister. "You know I don't! Once her kids are back in school,

Marsha wants to work for us again. I can do watering and suchlike in the morning, and then take over when I get home after school every day, just like I did last fall."

"Last fall," he said, sounding implacable, "we didn't make enough money to justify having an employee."

"Business keeps picking up…."

"Does it? What did we make today?"

Her mouth opened and closed. She clearly didn't want to say, and Charlotte knew the day's receipts were pitiful. Most of the drivers who'd pulled in had wanted some of the early corn, but at five ears for a dollar, the corn wasn't that profitable. And the Russells were no longer growing enough of it to make it profitable; not nearly enough, for example, to sell it to one of the frozen-food processors. Back when the farm was a going concern, Daddy had grown both corn and peas for frozen-food packers, but times had changed. He didn't have enough acreage compared to huge farm conglomerates. He'd gone to selling locally to grocery stores, adding strawberries and raspberries, but there was too much competition from other small farms, the strawberries were labor intensive to pick, and one year some kind of rust had wiped out the raspberries. All three of them knew the harsh realities. Faith's plan had been a last-ditch hope, staving off the inevitable for over a year now.

"We never do as well with everyone thinking back-to-school. Come September..."

"It's time for us to think about selling," he said, his gruff voice becoming gentler.

Faith shot to her feet. "No! Small businesses take time to build. You know that! So today was slow. Weekends we're hustling nonstop. Aren't we, Char?"

Charlotte nodded, even though she knew how many of those weekend customers ended up buying no more than a couple of pots of petunias or a single jar of jam. People enjoyed browsing the antiques, but they rarely bought. Faith had admitted that the armoire and the table were the only furniture sales in the past month. The maze, Charlotte thought, would bring in money, and the pumpkins ripening in the field beyond the barn would be popular, but once Halloween was past she couldn't imagine the farm drawing any business until close to Christmas. And would anyone at all stop in January, or February, or March? Seasonal sales were all very well when they were adequate to carry a business over the dead time, but theirs weren't. And Christmas tree farmers, for example, didn't pay an employee year-round, which Faith had been doing.

"I'm just asking you to think about it," Dad

said. The ruddy tones of his skin color were turning gray again, Charlotte was dismayed to see. He fumbled for a button and pushed. The bed whirred, the head of it lowering. He didn't let it go far. Now he was reaching for the bottle of pain pills and then the glass of iced tea, though the ice had long since melted.

Faith started to rise again, but at his glare she sank back down on the sofa. Her expression was so well controlled, it might have been carved from marble, but shame and anguish seemed to be seeping from her pores. Charlotte could *feel* her misery. She'd almost forgotten how she could once do that, just as Faith knew immediately when she was in turmoil. Charlotte would have sworn, back then, that she would know if Faith was ever really in trouble even if they were hundreds of miles apart.

But she'd found out she was wrong. She hadn't had an inkling that her twin sister's husband was beating the crap out of her. She'd had no idea, even when she was home for the holidays and Rory and Faith were right here in the same room with her, sitting around the Christmas tree opening presents and sipping mulled cider as if everything was fine.

So maybe, Charlotte thought, *I'm wrong right now about what I think Faith is feeling.*

Only, she knew she wasn't. Just as she

knew—was afraid—that her sister wouldn't talk to her about it. She'd stand up, just as she was doing right now, and take her plate and Dad's as casually as if the meal had come to a natural end and now it was time to clean up.

"We don't have pie or anything, but we do have lime sherbet if anyone would like some," she said.

Charlotte rose, too, picking up her own plate. "Not me."

"Never did have a sweet tooth," their father grumbled, which was a flat-out lie. Oh, how he'd loved Mom's blueberry pie! Or her apple pie, warm with a big scoop of vanilla ice cream on top.

He'd lost weight since Mom died, Charlotte realized. Grown gaunt. Maybe pie didn't taste as good to him anymore. She had a flash of memory, Dad at Christmas dinner last year pushing away his plate without going back for seconds and declining the offer of pumpkin pie, another once-upon-a-time favorite of his.

Her heart cramped, and after following Faith to the kitchen, Charlotte asked in a low voice, "Does Dad go for regular checkups with his doctor? He didn't look good even before the accident, did he?"

"No," Faith said, "but I insisted...oh, two years ago, I think, that he get a thorough physical. They didn't find anything wrong with him. He's just..." She shrugged, not looking at her sister.

"If he was to sell the farm, what would he *do* with himself?" The idea of their father forcibly retired and idle was unimaginable. Watching him now, confined to a bed, was painful enough.

"I don't know," Faith whispered. She had set down the dirty dishes beside the sink and stood with her head bent, looking frail.

Had *she* lost weight? Charlotte had felt bony, even brittle, compared to her sister when she'd first arrived, but she knew she must be gaining weight. She'd been eating like a pig, maybe because she was physically active, maybe because the food here was just plain *better* than the microwavable stuff she usually subsisted on. But Faith's appetite hadn't been great, she realized, thinking back. Especially since the fire, she'd picked at the food on her plate.

Oh, good. Give them another few weeks, and they'd probably weigh exactly the same amount, as they frequently had when they took turns on the scale during their adolescence. Like all the other ways they were identical, Charlotte had abhorred not even being able to separate herself from her sister by a pound or two.

This time...well, this time what she felt was worry.

Chief Wheeler had damn well better find Rory

Hardesty and throw his ass in jail. She could talk to Gray, ask him to push Wheeler.

She heard his voice, gentle but utterly determined. *I'll call, Charlotte.*

Oh, damn. Closing her eyes, she pressed a hand to her chest. What would she say when he called, or the next time he stopped by? *Yeah, sure, kissing you could be fun, but, hey, let's not start anything when we both know I'll be outta here in just a few weeks?*

Reason said she could look at it as a summer fling. People did things like that when they were on vacation.

I can't! I just can't! It was a cry that came from deep inside her, where misery and panic grew, pressing at her rib cage until she felt she needed to wrap her arms around herself to contain it.

Gray could make her feel too much. She couldn't afford that. Because it would be temporary, and it would hurt when it ended. And because… She didn't know why. Only that this clawing fear felt something like her desperate need *not* to be an identical twin.

Not to be so intimate with another person that she couldn't pull away.

If he called—when he called—she would say, *Sorry, not interested.*

CHAPTER EIGHT

GRAY DID CALL THAT EVENING, even though his gut told him it was a mistake. Charlotte had a harder time saying no to his face. But he'd dropped by the farm casually so many times, he was running out of excuses. Anyway—shouldn't he be able to call and ask a woman on a date, like normal people did?

Faith answered and passed the phone to Charlotte, who said, "Hello, Gray," with deep reserve in her voice.

Gray pushed open the French doors to his back deck and stepped outside. "I just talked to Ben Wheeler. Hardesty isn't surfacing. Wheeler asked me to beg you two to consider getting a gun and learning to use it."

"Can you really picture either of us shooting someone?"

I think you could. The realization sprang into his mind, and he wasn't sure if he should tell her he believed she was capable of killing if she had to. Jaw tightening, Gray thought, *Yeah, she could do it, but then she'd fall apart.*

No, he didn't like the idea of either of the Russell sisters armed or—God forbid—having to defend themselves with a gun.

He cleared his throat. "Just passing on a message."

"Fine."

Silence.

He walked to the edge of the deck and gazed down at the river, running low with late summer. He usually considered himself a decent strategist; two years ago, he'd decided he wanted to be mayor and had set about taking the steps to make it happen. He'd done his best since he laid eyes on Charlotte Russell to back her into a corner and make her realize she wanted him. Unfortunately, this time he was well aware he was failing.

But, damn it, he had to ask. Turning his back on the river, he said, "Charlotte, will you have dinner with me one of these nights?"

She didn't even hesitate, which told him she'd prepared her answer. "Gray, it's not a good idea. I won't be in West Fork for long, and I'm not interested in short-term involvement."

Feeling desperate, he pointed out, "You had dinner with Wheeler."

This time, she was quiet for a moment. "That was…an impulse."

"You weren't really interested in him, were you? Which made him safe."

"Is that ego talking?" she challenged. "I must have the hots for you, or I wouldn't be saying no?"

"Only you can tell me that."

"Well, I'm not going to! Good night, Gray."

Dead air told him she'd hung up. He suspected that in the good old days she'd have slammed the phone down.

The fact that she was angry didn't surprise him. Charlotte clearly didn't like being vulnerable, and for some reason she feared that he had the capability of making her feel just that. But wasn't that part of falling in love? Hell, even of sex? Was she determined not to have either in her life?

He set his phone down and dropped into an Adirondack chair. Head back, he tried to let the cool evening air and the quiet of his aerie on the bluff above the river valley relax him.

It was time to give up on her. Whether he liked it or not, Charlotte had slammed the door in his face. He knew she was attracted to him; he'd felt her response hum through her when their lips had touched. He'd seen the flare of alarm whenever their eyes met. But that meant nothing if she was determined to shut him out.

And she was.

He'd known from the beginning that she was a complex and conflicted woman. He'd felt some primitive urge to soothe her, to make her life easier, to take care of her.

Well, she was having none of it.

Get over it, he told himself bleakly. *Stay away from the Russell farm.*

She'd be gone, back to California, before he knew it.

But the tension in his body didn't abate any more than the frustration in his gut. Forgetting about Charlotte Russell wasn't going to be easy. He wanted too badly to know what drove her, why she was afraid of him, and what it would be like to make love with her.

He also couldn't forget that Rory Hardesty was still out there, still angry. Or that Charlotte wasn't about to let the bastard get to Faith without going through her first.

A FEW DAYS LATER, CHARLOTTE persuaded Faith to leave her in charge.

"You know you should start getting your classroom ready for the first day of school. And you have meetings you have to attend some of the days. Today you can just concentrate on...whatever it is you do."

Faith smiled. "I decorate. When school lets out, we have to pack away everything. I've been assigned a different classroom this year. I need to cover the bulletin board with construction paper and put the alphabet stencils up. I make signs with the students' names to assign cubbies. I put books on the shelves, and plan some of the first projects and do whatever copying and cutting out has to be done in advance. I…"

Charlotte held up a hand. "Okay, I get the idea. Go. I'll be fine." When she saw that Faith was still hesitating, she said, "I have your cell-phone number if I need you. I can run to the house and check on Dad quickly when there aren't any customers. I'm a capable human being, I promise."

So Faith went, leaving Charlotte to chat with customers, to ring up a handful of purchases, to water the perennials, annuals and shrubs in pots outside. To dash to the house several times only to find Dad sleeping or watching TV. And, when she had nothing else to do, to stare at the pages of a thriller she'd picked up at the San Francisco airport.

Of course, every time she picked up the book, instead of actually being able to concentrate on the words, she stewed.

Her list of worries had grown and metamorphosed since the call from Faith that had brought Charlotte home.

Rory had been, and still was, at the top, of course. He'd clearly gone off the deep end, and Charlotte hoped Police Chief Ben Wheeler understood that. She was irritated that he hadn't been by the farm or called either her or Faith in days. Gray's secondhand reports weren't an adequate substitute, and even he'd been absent since Charlotte had declined to go out to dinner with him.

Dad was healing, if more slowly than he liked, which was a relief. His state of mind was another story, though. He'd lost all the determination that made him the man she once knew. Unlike Faith, Charlotte could imagine life without the farm still being here as a home-base; what she *couldn't* imagine was her father without the farm. He didn't know how to do anything else! He'd never been interested in taking cruises, or going to Hawaii or even out to dinner in Everett—never mind Seattle. His idea of a high time was playing bingo at the church hall or going to pancake breakfasts at the grange. He had friends, a few other crusty farmers—or, at least, he'd *had* friends. Charlotte frowned. She'd noticed a new gas station and minimart out near the freeway where the O'Brien farm had once been. And the Guthries' house still stood, but the fields surrounding it were strangled by weeds and blackberry bushes. Were the Guthries even there anymore?

And then there was Faith, who, having lost her dream of husband and family, was unwilling even to think about her childhood home going under the bulldozer. She was tough, she'd survive. But she would be further diminished if she failed to hold on to the farm. Faith, Charlotte knew, had always been fragile in a way she herself wasn't. There'd been times the knowledge of that fragility made Charlotte angry, mostly as a cover for her guilt. Because, of course, Faith had been losing her twin sister, too, from the time they reached kindergarten age.

Finally, somewhere at the bottom of her list, Charlotte had to acknowledge her own problems. She needed to make a decision about finding a new job. She had scanned job-listing sites online, but hadn't sent out a résumé since coming home. In the meantime, a whopping mortgage payment would be automatically withdrawn from her account on September 1. She would have to put her condo on the market, and soon. Even if she found another job in the Bay Area, it was likely to be in San Jose or Palo Alto, more of a commute than she'd want to make. Selling it could well take a good long while, given the recession, and every month that mortgage payment would take another whack out of her limited savings.

But she wasn't ready to go back to San Francisco, even long enough to list the condo. How could she leave while Rory was still out there, plotting how he could hurt Faith? Or while Dad was confined to a hospital bed in the living room? Or, for that matter, when her departure would mean that Faith would have to pay for help she couldn't afford?

For the first time, she acknowledged openly to herself that she was considering staying in Washington for good. She could find a job in the software industry here as easily as the Bay Area. She might not want to live in West Fork, but she'd be close by if Dad or Faith needed her. She'd feel…rooted in a way she hadn't since she left home.

Charlotte reluctantly added Mayor Gray Van Dusen to her list, since she'd been failing to keep herself from thinking about him, about his smiles and his kiss. A relationship with him wouldn't be impossible if she moved back to the area. She was trying very hard, though, to believe that he wasn't part of the equation she was juggling when making a decision about her future. The idea of never seeing him again scared her almost as much as the idea of getting involved with him did. Neither possibility loosened the knot that had lodged in her chest almost from the moment she'd met him, and that had ached ever since.

I'm a mess, she mourned. *Would he even want me if he knew?*

It infuriated her that she couldn't dismiss thoughts of him like she would a job listing that was briefly appealing but ultimately didn't meet her needs. She'd always been able to put men out of her mind! No one had ever been important enough to make him linger despite her best efforts. *Why Gray?* she asked herself.

Because of his smile, which was gentle and somehow knowing and impossibly sexy? And the thoughtful way he looked at her with those gray eyes, as though he saw deep inside her where she was confused and frightened and needy?

Oh, God, she thought. *I've missed him these past few days. So much.*

And she'd pretty much told him to get lost.

Charlotte was so grateful when a car pulled in off the highway, she jumped off her stool behind the counter and strolled out, even though the people probably just wanted to pick out five ears of corn from the wagonful out front. She grimaced. Yep, another fifty cents of profit for the Russell operation.

But the couple who got out of the car ignored the corn and wandered in, the woman heading for the arts and crafts, the husband asking, "Do you sell any Japanese maples?"

Glad she at least knew what a maple leaf looked like, Charlotte left the woman to her own devices and led the husband to the rows of tree saplings, where Faith did indeed offer half a dozen varieties of Japanese maple. Most were red-leafed, one had vivid green leaves and yet another had cream and pale green variegated foliage. She stole a look at the price tags and blinked. Did people really pay that much for a tree still so frail it could be snapped off if the family German shepherd leaned on it?

"I'd like five of the same variety," the man said. "We just bought a place with no yard in yet except for a front lawn. I intend to plant them in a row along the street. Do you know which one has the best fall color? And do you have five of any one of these?"

"I'm told they all have spectacular fall color," Charlotte assured him, echoing what she'd heard Faith telling a customer the other day. "And yes, we have more out in our wholesale area." She hoped.

Faith kept a small library of gardening books behind the counter inside, and Charlotte was able to find one that described the particular virtues of a number of the maple hybrids.

Having given it to him to read, she went back into the barn to find the wife oohing and aahing over a circa 1880 walnut bedroom set that had become available after a very elderly woman in town had died. The original dark finish was in good shape, and the set included footboard and headboard, bedside stand, tallboy dresser and armoire. Faith had priced the lot at $2,000, a steal by antique store standards, but a whole lot of money by Russell Family Farm standards.

Wishing for a moment that she *did* have a helper, Charlotte finally gambled on their honesty and excused herself to race out to the back forty to verify that yes indeed, they could supply five of either of the two varieties of maple the man was still weighing.

And when she got back, it was to find that the woman had dragged the man in to study the bedroom set.

Ten minutes later, she rang up a sale that totalled $2,500 plus tax. Kenneth Engelhart promised to be back the next morning with a U-Haul truck to pick up the walnut bedroom set and five potted Oshio-Beni maples with bright red-orange, delicately serrated leaves.

Smiling, she saw them out, chatted with some people buying corn and waited on two women who browsed for half an hour before buying one of Faith's hand-painted Welcome signs and a flat of pansies.

She was back to reading the thriller when she saw Faith drive in and park by the house. When her sister walked into the barn a minute later, Charlotte lifted her head.

"Hey. Take a look at the bedroom set."

Faith stopped, turned and gaped at the Sold tag hanging from the footboard. Her mouth was still hanging open when she spun back to face

Charlotte. "How much did you have to come down?"

Charlotte dropped the book and grinned. "They didn't even try to bargain."

A disbelieving laugh erupted out of Faith's throat. Then she clapped her hand over her mouth. Behind it, she was chortling.

"And—get this—they bought five Japanese maples, too. A twenty-five-hundred-dollar sale!" She danced her way around the end of the counter and to Faith, grabbing her hands. "Man, it was fun. I wish you'd been here!"

Faith let out a belly laugh and began to dance, too. "Oh, my God. Oh, my God!"

Somewhere during their celebration, it occurred to Charlotte that she hadn't bubbled with happiness like this in…years. It had to be years. In designing software, triumphs were incremental. There was hardly ever a huge leap of inspiration and accomplishment that could make her laugh out loud.

This…this *joy,* she thought, was because the one big sale made it possible to hope again. And she'd done something that really mattered to Faith, and maybe to Dad. Best of all, she wasn't dancing and laughing alone.

Still clasping both of her sister's hands, Charlotte said, "I've missed you."

Faith's smile faded. Her face softened for a

moment, a too-fleeting one, before she wrapped herself in caution and reserve as though they were a blanket tugged close at night. She said quietly, "I've always missed you," and then turned away. "I'll do the last watering if you'll close out the cash register."

Happiness congealing, becoming something thick and lumpy and uncomfortable, Charlotte said, "Sure." She didn't watch as her twin left the barn, a momentary dark silhouette against the bright square of sunlight before disappearing outside.

Charlotte had never been so achingly aware that she'd done too much damage for them to be able to go back to a time when they'd been a unit.

It was my choice, she knew.

She wished she was the only one paying the price, that Faith hadn't been hurt, too. Charlotte didn't understand why, now, she had begun to regret the decision she'd made to sever a relationship she'd once believed reduced her to half a person, that left her terrified that even her thoughts and dreams weren't her own.

Standing still right where her sister had left her, Charlotte thought with some shock, *I don't believe that anymore. I am myself. Faith is herself. We may look alike, but we're not alike under the skin, where it counts.*

Maybe, just maybe, she'd *needed* the ten years away from home and her sister to discover who she was aside from an identical twin. But being home again also reminded her of how much she'd lost when she wrenched herself free.

There was no going back.

Would she also come to regret pushing Gray away out of a fear that felt uncomfortably similar?

THAT EVENING, FAITH BUBBLED about the miraculous sale and, when they went upstairs to bed, startled Charlotte with a quick hug and a murmured "Thanks," before they split off to their separate bedrooms.

Charlotte was surprised to realize that needing her was disconcerting Faith. Everything about their relationship these days seemed to trip them up, as if they were so busy dancing out of each other's way, they were instead constantly stepping on each other's feet and stubbing toes.

She went to bed feeling a little better. Difficult didn't mean impossible. Maybe they *could* save the farm. Maybe she and Faith could become friends. Truly sisters. Faith, Charlotte thought gratefully, would be better at forgiveness than she'd have been in her sister's place.

Faith relaxed with Charlotte as the week went

on, and even Dad's mood improved. Business was better, and they had all regained some hope.

The gray tinge disappeared from Dad's skin tone, and he got out of bed more easily. He was becoming more adept with the crutches, too. He admitted he had cut his daytime pain meds in half and was glad to feel less muddled.

Gray didn't call or come by. He had taken her at her word, which made her more miserable than she'd believed possible. Ben did phone once and gave Faith a clipped report.

"No news," she said, her face revealing none of the distress she must feel at his retreat.

Creep, Charlotte thought, even though she knew she was being a hypocrite. *She'd* hurt her sister more than Ben ever could.

She found herself more restless every night. She'd never needed as much sleep as Faith did—that was one thing that had made them different from the very beginning. Mom had said that Charlotte's naps were always shorter than Faith's, and she gave them up altogether much sooner than her sister did. But this restlessness was something more. The worries that she kept pushing down were shoving their way back up again, but refused to present themselves tidily one by one.

Gray's voice, somber rather than mocking as

she would have expected it to be: *Only you can tell me that.*

Faith saying, *I've always missed you,* making Charlotte remember the expression on her sister's face the day she'd announced that she wanted her own bedroom.

Dad, revealing himself as grim and seemingly hopeless however he might have hidden his unhappiness since the night he'd said he thought it was time to sell out.

Rory… What would he do next?

It was Rory who kept her awake. These past few days, she could all but *feel* him out there, with a prickling sense that it was only a matter of time before he attacked again.

When? she wondered, and flipped over in bed.

Despite the open window and the small fan she had running at the foot of the bed, Charlotte felt hot and sticky. She wished for rain, then made a face and unwished it. She had no idea how the corn maze would stand up to a serious summer storm. The air felt like there ought to be one, though—too sultry. She imagined the hairs on her arms prickling with electricity in the atmosphere, and she listened to the quiet as though thunder would rumble through it any minute.

Ugh, what a mood! Disgusted with herself, she got up and went to stand at the window for a minute, savoring the cool air. It was hot only inside, no surprise when the day's heat was trapped here upstairs. Hoping she wouldn't wake Faith, Charlotte padded silently down the hall without turning on the light.

Stepping into the shower, she started with lukewarm water and gradually adjusted it to cool and finally to flat-out, teeth-chattering cold. She was actually shivering when she stepped out, which felt fabulous. A minute later, a towel wrapping her wet hair, she opened the bathroom door and reached back for the light switch.

At a whisper of movement, her pulse leaped into overdrive, zero to sixty in under a second.

"You knew I'd be back, didn't you, bitch?" snarled the man materializing out of the darkness.

She started to whirl back toward the bathroom before thinking, *Oh God, Faith.* The bathroom door might lock, but Faith's bedroom door didn't.

Too late, anyway.

In the band of light from the bathroom she saw the knife Rory gripped and the rage that twisted his face.

She had no time to evade him. He slammed her into the door frame, a guttural sound escaping his throat. Someone was screaming. She drove her knee toward his groin and felt it connect instead with the solid bulk of thigh muscle. The backhand of his fist smashed into her cheek, and her head, buffered only by the towel, cracked against the frame. Charlotte's vision misted and her knees sagged, but she kept fighting.

Pain sliced her shoulder. The knife. God, had he stabbed her? She staggered backward into the bathroom, just enough to open space between them, then put everything she had into a kick that connected this time.

Bellowing, he almost fell. Crashed backward against the wall next to Faith's now open bedroom door. Holding a baseball bat in her hands, Faith stood in the opening, yelling.

Caught in the light from the bathroom, the knife in his hand red with her blood, Rory didn't seem to have noticed Faith. He was staring at Charlotte with shock. Not at her face—at her hair, dyed dark. The towel had fallen off.

"It was supposed to be her," he said hoarsely.

Downstairs, Dad bellowed, "The police are coming!"

Rory gave a wild look over his shoulder.

Some devil made Charlotte taunt him. "Disappointed it's me? Or do you want to kill me, too?"

Faith stepped out of the bedroom. Her expression was wild. She screamed, "I'm here, Rory." She jiggled the bat, warming up. "Come and get me."

Like the coward he was, he broke and ran. No, hobbled by Charlotte's last kick, he was bent over as he crashed down the stairs.

Gripping the door frame, Charlotte waited for the pounding of his running feet to reach the back of the house. The back door and screen to bang.

And then, in slow motion, unable to prevent it, she felt herself fold up and collapse to the floor, her cheek coming to rest on the hall carpet. The last thing she saw before she passed out was her sister's terrified face, inches from hers; the last thing she heard was Faith's voice, though she was past making out words.

No, Charlotte thought hazily—she heard a siren, too.

THE FIRST RING OF THE TELEPHONE had Gray rearing up in bed, heart slamming, before he realized what had awakened him. Groaning, he reached for the phone.

"Van Dusen."

"Wheeler here." The police chief's voice was taut. "One of my officers just called. Hardesty broke into the Russells' place tonight. Charlotte's hurt. The EMTs are already there, and Cooper says they're rushing her to the hospital. I'm on my way to the farm right now."

"How bad?" Gray asked, his voice nobody's he recognized.

"I don't know. Just that she's unconscious." He paused. "There's a knife wound."

Swearing, more scared than he could ever remember being, he was already pulling on jeans. "I'm on my way to the hospital. You'll be there?"

"After I talk to Faith and their father."

"Nobody's with Charlotte?"

"They don't usually let anyone ride along in the ambulance."

In the act of pulling a shirt over his head, Gray hung up the phone.

God. He'd known it would come to this.

It occurred to him as he snatched his keys and wallet from the dresser top that Wheeler hadn't said whether Rory was safely handcuffed in the back of the first responding officer's car.

He ascended the stairs two at a time and was backing out of the garage within a minute of snapping his cell phone shut. The idea of Charlotte at the hospital without anyone who cared about her made him sick. Was Faith hurt, too? Or just too shaken up to drive herself?

Or—*hell*—did she think she couldn't leave her father?

Ignoring speed limits, it still took Gray ten minutes from his river-bluff home to reach the small community hospital on the other side of town. The visitors' lot was deserted at this time of night, so he was able to park close to the emergency entrance. He raced in and said to the nurse behind the counter, "Charlotte Russell."

"I believe they may have her in X-ray, Mayor. Let me check."

She lifted her phone, dialed and spoke quietly. He stood absolutely still, adrenaline rocketing through him. He wanted to lunge across the counter and grab the goddamn phone out of her hand.

Hanging up, she said, "If you want to speak to her doctor, I'm afraid you'll have to wait until he's reviewed her films."

"I want to see her," Gray said roughly.

"She's still up in X-ray." More cautiously, she asked, "And, er, are you a family member?" Her eyes widened at his expression. "Ah…I'll have the doctor come speak to you as soon as possible."

He couldn't sit. He paced the otherwise empty waiting room, hands balled into fists in his jeans' pockets to keep him from smashing one of them into a wall. He'd never felt such violent impulses before. And the fear, it curled deep in his gut, expanding as each minute dragged into the next and he imagined… God. The worst. Charlotte dying back there while he prowled uselessly out here. Her blood dripping onto the floor. Her face, milk pale, slack without the force of her personality animating it, her lids covering her vivid blue eyes.

He turned at the sound of the swinging door, his tension jumping another notch.

"Mayor?" The E.R. doc was only a few years older than Gray, although already balding. They'd played a round of golf together at a charity tournament just two months ago. "I understand you're here because of Ms. Russell?"

"Yes." What the hell was his name? Steven. Steven something.

"She has no family here yet?"

"No. Just me."

Nolan. Steve Nolan. That was it.

"And your relationship to Ms. Russell?" Dr. Nolan asked delicately.

"We're seeing each other," Gray lied. Hell; literally, it wasn't a lie. Or hadn't been a lie, until this past week. "Chief Wheeler called me as soon as he heard. He knew..." Gray stopped, his throat closing.

"Ah." The doc's face relaxed. "Well, she's regained consciousness and seems lucid, so I imagine she'd like to have someone she knows at her side." He half laughed. "I've met Faith. Amazing how much she and her sister look alike, isn't it? One of the nurses says they're identical twins."

"Yes." What the hell difference did it make? He said urgently, "Wheeler said she was stabbed."

Nolan shook his head. "Sliced. There was a lot of blood, but the cut's fairly shallow. We were more worried about a head injury. He punched her face, and then her head got slammed back against a door frame, which tend to be pretty solid in those old houses. She's got quite a goose egg on the back of her head and she's definitely concussed. We'll be keeping her overnight at a minimum. I'm about to put some stitches in that cut, and unless she objects I don't see why you can't be there."

Gray scrubbed a hand across his face. "I want to be there."

The doctor clapped a hand on his back and steered him through the swinging doors.

Gray had toured the hospital after he took office. He knew there were two emergency operating rooms back here and a dozen cubicles. In passing, he glanced into one where the curtain was partially pushed back and saw a woman cradling a sobbing toddler.

"Ear infection," Nolan murmured.

The other curtains were closed. Gray heard no voices, nothing but the crying child. At the last cubicle, the doctor pulled back the curtain, mentioned something about being back in a few minutes and let Gray step in alone, his attention riveted on the woman lying utterly still on the narrow bed. Her eyes were closed, and her face…

The fury rose in him like a tsunami, swamping every other emotion until it receded enough for him to breathe again.

One side of her face was swollen and already purple. She wouldn't be able to open that eye even if she wanted to.

A sound escaped him. He couldn't help it.

Charlotte stirred, turned her head on the pillow and moaned. One eye opened a crack. "Gray," she whispered, and suddenly tears slid down her cheeks.

He wasn't even conscious of taking the steps to reach her side, only that he was there, gripping her hand, wiping her tears away with his knuckle on the one cheek he dared touch.

"I'm so sorry we didn't stop him in time. So damn sorry," he said. "I should have kept sleeping on the couch."

He thought she chuckled, but then she whimpered again because it had hurt. "I wasn't exactly…welcoming," she whispered.

"I shouldn't have let that stop me."

"Faith… Is she all right?"

"As far as I know. I imagine she'll be along

once she gets your dad settled. Wheeler's out there talking to them."

"My head hurts."

"Yeah." He gently brushed her hair back from her forehead and realized it was spiky and wet. "It's going to hurt for a while."

"He got in the house."

"I know."

"He thought I was Faith." Her whisper was so faint he had to bend over to hear her, but she seemed to be driven by the need to tell him what happened. "I took a shower. I had a towel wrapped around my head." One slender hand lifted as if she were going to gesture, then fell back atop the white blanket. "He had a knife."

The fear in Gray's gut curled, snake-like. As if he were watching it on video, he saw her coming out of the bathroom, finding Rory Hardesty waiting in the hall with a knife in his hand. It was a miracle she wasn't dead.

"At home," she whispered, "I do kickboxing."

Another time, he might have laughed. Trust Charlotte to kickbox instead of stair-stepping or doing aerobics in pink leotards.

"I knew you'd fight." He couldn't seem to keep his hands off her. One enveloped hers. The other cradled her face while his thumb moved over her uninjured cheek, stroking, stroking, feeling the delicacy of her bones and the satin of her skin, the lingering moisture. "Hardesty is a fool," Gray said harshly.

Her lips actually curved. "Faith came charging out of her bedroom with a baseball bat. You wouldn't have recognized her."

"I'm glad to hear she's got it in her."

"She's…tough." It was barely more than a sigh.

God. God. His chest ached. All he could think was, *Charlotte isn't as tough as she wanted to believe she was.* Hardesty *hurt* her. The son of a bitch hurt her.

"Ah, sweetheart," he murmured, the pad of his thumb finding her mouth with all the tenderness he felt.

Quick footsteps sounded in the hall. They came faster and faster, breaking into a run. Then the curtains were shoved back with a rattle of the rings, and Faith all but flew into the cubicle.

"Charlotte! Oh, no! Charlotte."

A sob erupted from Charlotte and, the next second, her sister was hugging her with exquisite care.

Gray was aware of Wheeler standing there watching the reunion. Charlotte's hand squirmed free from Gray's so she could embrace her sister, cheek pressed to cheek.

Feeling empty—no, bereft—he stepped back. She didn't need him anymore, now that Faith was here. Why had he thought anything had changed?

CHAPTER NINE

IT WAS STUPID TO FEEL EXTRANEOUS AND—damn it!—jealous just because Charlotte now had Faith here to hold her sister's hand.

He needed to talk to Wheeler anyway, find out whether Hardesty was in custody. He glanced at the police chief, who jerked his head toward the hall.

But when Gray took another step away, Charlotte's head rolled on the pillow and her blue eye fastened on him with alarm.

"Are you...are you leaving?"

The jealousy faded and he felt... Oh, hell, like an even bigger idiot than before. But that wasn't all he felt. Something that had been cramped in his chest almost from the day they met eased.

He shook his head, smiling a little. "No. I'm not going anywhere."

Faith had straightened to look at him and then down at her sister, her face a study in... He wasn't quite sure.

Charlotte swallowed. "You don't have to..."

"Yeah, I do," he said softly.

"Oh." More tears leaked from her eyes, the one gazing at him as if she didn't want to let him out of her sight, the other even more swollen than it had been when he'd first arrived. "Thank you," she whispered, the words bumpy.

"I'm going to go talk to Ben," he said. "And then I'll be right back to hold your hand while Dr. Nolan stitches you up."

"Oh, boy. That sounds like fun."

There was his Charlotte, trying to be peevish even when she didn't have the spirit to actually grumble.

The fact that she was able to make the attempt allowed him to smile again as he left the cubicle and followed Wheeler out to the still empty waiting room. Wheeler glanced at the nurse behind the counter and kept walking, through the automatic doors and outside where the night was cool and sharp.

Gray's smile was long gone by the time they faced each other at the curb where the ambulance had earlier unloaded Charlotte.

"Tell me Hardesty is in custody."

Ben Wheeler shook his head, his fingers stabbing into his hair as if he wanted to yank it out. "Goddamn it, no. He'd disappeared by the time the first unit rolled in. He might have been hiding out there, but we couldn't find him or his truck."

Gray let an obscenity escape. "I'll kill him myself if you don't get your hands on him first."

Wheeler gave him a dark look. "You know better than that."

"Yeah? You would have just read him his rights tonight if you'd found him ducked down behind the tractor?"

The muscles in his police chief's jaw spasmed. It took him a minute before he said tonelessly, "I'd have done my job."

Fury and fear seething in him, Gray stepped forward until they were toe-to-toe. "Then do it," he snapped. "So far, I've got to tell you, I'm disappointed in you."

Wheeler's eyes burned. After a minute he turned away, flattened both hands on the rough stucco wall of the hospital and bent his head, breathing hard.

Gray knew he wasn't being fair, but fairness was beyond him tonight. He'd brought in a big-city cop to make *his* town safer, and that new police chief couldn't even stop one stalker. Couldn't keep two vulnerable women from being hurt.

No, fairness was beyond him.

He turned and walked back into the hospital, the doors whooshing open and then shut behind him.

The nurse let him through the inner doors. The mother and toddler were gone, he realized, and no other business had arrived. This was a quiet night in the E.R. He stepped into Charlotte's cubicle to find that the doctor was already setting stitches in the long, ugly gash that ran from her upper arm to a place well below her collarbone.

Shallow? Gray thought, staring in unwilling horror. He couldn't imagine it wouldn't leave a scar to remind her of the terrifying encounter. If the knife had bit any deeper…

He clenched his teeth together and lifted his gaze to Charlotte's battered face to find her watching him. Faith held her hand, but from that moment on Charlotte never looked away from Gray, standing at the foot of the bed. Not once, while Nolan applied stitches, not until he'd covered his work with dressings and let the nurse lift the hospital gown into place and tie it again behind her neck.

Gray scarcely breathed, holding that gaze, trying to send comfort and strength even though he wasn't touching her. The anger he hid, knowing that wasn't what she needed right now.

By the time Nolan was done, Gray could tell Charlotte was getting fuzzy. He was glad when an orderly arrived to wheel her upstairs to a room. Faith and Gray both followed. Gray didn't know what had happened to Wheeler, or whether he'd brought Faith in, leaving her with no way to get home again.

He asked quietly, when they were instructed to wait in the hall while Charlotte was shifted to the new bed and settled.

"I drove myself," Faith said. "Chief Wheeler followed me."

"You look at the end of your rope." He hadn't noticed earlier, but now he saw the tremors and the shock in her eyes and the way she swayed on her feet. "You need to get some sleep."

"I don't know if I can." She bit her lip so hard he was surprised she didn't draw blood. "I'm going to get a gun and learn to shoot it. He is never, *ever* going to threaten us like that again." The steel in her voice crumpled at the end. "I will never forgive myself for this…."

"Yourself?" Gray caught her upper arm. "What are you talking about? This isn't your fault, Faith. You didn't make that bastard what he is. He fooled you early on, and you were smart enough to get out. You're not responsible for his craziness!"

"I married him."

"Was he *ever* violent before the wedding?"

She let out a shaky breath and shook her head.

"Then tell me. How were you supposed to know?"

"I don't know!" she all but screamed at him. "I don't know! But I should have! I should have..."

He reached out to her, but Wheeler, appearing from nowhere, shouldered him aside with one angry look and wrapped her in his arms. Gray found himself staring at the police chief's back. He could just hear Wheeler's murmur, oddly gentle and rough at the same time.

"No, no. There was no way you could know. You can't blame yourself, Faith. You can't."

The nurse stepped out of Charlotte's room and said, "You can come in now," but Faith didn't seem to hear.

Gray left them in the hallway and went in. Once again his heart cramped at the sight of Charlotte looking defeated, the battered half of her face hidden under an ice pack. He pulled up the room's one chair and took her hand.

She squinted at him from her good eye and mumbled, "Gray," then sighed, "Oh, good." He'd have sworn she was asleep a second later, as if she'd waited to let go until he was there.

He couldn't avoid the knowledge that the attraction he'd felt for her, the frustration and fascination and hunger to protect her, had all coalesced into an emotion bigger than anything he'd ever experienced.

Love.

With a woman who refused to go out to dinner with him. Oh, yeah—he was permanently, deeply, foolishly in love with her, and he had no idea what would come of it.

What he did know was, he wouldn't be leaving her side anytime soon.

CHARLOTTE HAD NO IDEA HOW long she'd been asleep, or what awakened her, only that the smell, the feel of the bed, jarred her with the awareness that she wasn't anywhere familiar.

She jerked, then moaned as the St. Helens of all headaches threatened to blow open the top of her skull.

"Hey," a man's voice murmured. "Sshh. Lie still."

Gentle fingers stroked her forehead, and despite the command she tipped her face toward that hand.

Oh, God. She could hardly see at all. What was wrong? Charlotte lifted a shaking hand to the explosion of pain at her cheekbone.

"Wha' hap...pened?" she managed to ask.

"Rory." The voice was still soft, but somehow grim at the same time. "He attacked you."

It came back to her in Technicolor. The rage, the knife, the shock when her towel fell to the floor. Her own helpless inability, once he fled, to keep from slipping bonelessly to the floor herself.

"Gray," she tried to say. Her tongue was sticking to the roof of her mouth. Her lips felt cracked.

"Would you like a drink of water?"

She started to nod and immediately regretted it.

Gray slid an arm behind her, lifting her just enough for her to sip. When she was done, he settled her back against the pillows as carefully, then pushed the button to summon the nurse.

She demonstrated her lucidity and was awarded more pain meds. Clinging to her last moments of wakefulness, Charlotte whispered, "You're still here."

She could just make him out, sitting up in the chair at the bedside, his elbows resting on his knees, one hand covering hers. It should bother her—shouldn't it—that out of all the people she knew it was Gray Van Dusen who wouldn't leave her to awaken alone in the hospital. Tomorrow she might let herself be alarmed by how *right* it felt to have him here.

"I told you I wasn't going anywhere," he said, his voice deep and slow and serious.

"Did they catch Rory?"

He was silent long enough to give away the

answer before he admitted it aloud. "No. But they will. This time, he showed his face."

Yes. Oh, yes, she'd seen his face.

She heard herself mumble, "Okay," and felt his thumb moving on the back of her hand as she slid into sleep as if it were dark, still water.

Gray was there the next time she woke up, too, and the time after, when morning light let her see him better. Slouched low in the chair, he was asleep when she first opened her eyes—no, her *eye*. His sun-streaked hair was tousled and tending to spikiness. Dark blond stubble shadowed his jaw. He didn't look as defenseless as he ought to in sleep, or as young, not with frown lines between his brows, and his mouth compressed.

She hadn't moved at all, only lay studying him, but suddenly he was looking back at her, aware and alert with no seeming transition between sleep and wakefulness. Their gazes held, as if… She didn't know. As if they were each searching for something.

"How's the head?" he asked, after a minute.

"Like the Fourth of July finale. Complete with the 1812 Overture blaring out of cheap speakers. I'm afraid to move."

"You look…" He fumbled for a word. "Better."

"You mean, like hell."

A smile creased his cheeks. "That, too. But also completely in the here and now."

"Umm." She thought. "You did say that Rory got away."

"Unfortunately." The one word came out as a rumble. He didn't let his expression change, but Charlotte heard his anger.

"Bastard."

Gray's mouth tilted up again. "I'd have said worse." He paused. "Your sister says she's going to buy that gun and learn how to use it."

"Faith?" The surprise in her voice was tempered the instant she remembered the sight of her twin emerging from the bedroom with the baseball bat poised to swing. "I'll believe it when I see it," she said anyway. "But then…"

"Then?"

"She's changed."

"You probably have, too."

"Since I came home…" She shifted, a kind of itch running under her skin. Discomfort. She *was* changing, hour by hour, and she didn't know what to make of it or where it would end.

She must have looked fretful, because Gray rose to his feet and smoothed her hair back, then stroked her cheek. "Shall I call the nurse?"

"Not yet. As long as I don't move my head…"

He chuckled, the honeyed rumble that

had gotten her into trouble in the corn maze. "Does this hurt?" He massaged her temple, her cheekbone.

"No," she whispered, letting her eye close. "It feels good."

Almost unbearably good. He liked to touch, it seemed, and knew how. It had been so long since anyone had touched her like this, not with passion but rather with…caring.

Now his whole hand moved down to wrap and squeeze her nape, a rhythmic massage that dragged a throaty moan from her.

His fingers stilled briefly, then resumed the massage that would have had her arching her back to give him better access if only she hadn't been too afraid to move.

She felt a light touch again on her face. His other hand, she supposed, as she savored the incredibly light brush of fingertips across her cheekbone, down along her jaw, up to her mouth.

Except she realized, then, that it was his lips skimming over her face. His lips, settling over hers. Not demanding, not expecting any response, just…soothing. Exploring, perhaps. No longer breathing, suspended in wonder at the sweetness of this kiss, Charlotte thought she felt the warm, damp flick of his tongue.

But then his mouth glided back to her jaw, and

up to nuzzle her earlobe, then came to rest at her temple, where his breath stirred her hair.

"Ah, Charlotte," he whispered. "I was so scared last night."

"I'm sorry," she whispered back.

This chuckle was a warm puff against her skin. "Not your fault."

"No." Oh, this was probably a huge mistake, but she had to say it anyway. "I mean, that I said no."

His stillness was absolute this time. She had to crack her eyelid open to see what he was thinking.

He'd lifted his head and was staring at her. "Does that mean you'll have dinner with me?" he asked carefully.

"Yes. When I can appear in public without scaring people."

After a minute, he said, "It's a date." He grinned at her. "You, Charlotte, have a gift for surprising me."

She went for a snort, soft enough not to jar her head. "Despite having my life flashing before my eyes, I avoided any major epiphanies. This is the sum total."

Now he was laughing. "*Did* your life flash before your eyes?"

"No, only deep regret that *I* wasn't the one holding the baseball bat."

Another delighted laugh, another gentle-as-air kiss, and he reached for the call button. "Time to rise and shine, sweetheart."

He ended up getting shunted aside in the next hour or two, between Faith's arrival and then the doctor's. Not Dr. Nolan—he had presumably worked the graveyard shift and was now home sacked out. This was a Dr. Bjorback, the morning trauma specialist, a sturdy tank of a woman with a no-nonsense style that suited Charlotte. The doctor shone lights into her eyes, and established once again that she remembered what had happened, what day it was and where she was. She swallowed another pill, which muffled the pain enough to allow her to struggle upright and to shuffle to the bathroom. Dr. Bjorback decided she could go home, so long as she had family to hover over her.

Gray insisted on driving her. "My car actually has shock absorbers," he told Faith.

Charlotte was alert enough to be amused. He must have seen Faith's aging Blazer bounding over the potholes in their hard-packed dirt driveway.

Faith, bless her, had brought Charlotte some real clothes, including a bra and capri-length pants instead of the skimpy poplin boxer shorts she'd worn to bed last night.

She was taken to the curbside in a wheelchair,

and placed so tenderly in Gray's Prius that she had only one moment of swirling light-headedness. The door had already been closed, and the nurse was turning to go back into the hospital, but Gray noticed and was swearing when he got in behind the wheel.

"They should have kept you another day."

"Just because my head hurts?"

"Because you look like you're going to pass out any minute," he snapped.

"The doctor said to expect some dizziness."

Gray grumbled anyway.

Halfway home, Charlotte let out a pained laugh. "Oh, poor Faith! Now she has *two* invalids on her hands! Maybe I should just crawl in next to Daddy, so she can spoon-feed us in tandem."

He shot her a quick look. "I can stay."

"Don't be silly. You hardly slept at all and you have two jobs waiting for you."

"They can keep waiting."

"Gray, I was kidding. You know I'll do nothing but sleep. And Dad's getting around better all the time. Besides, give me a couple of days and I'll be as good as new. Except for—" she reached up and tentatively touched her swollen cheek "—some garish side effects."

He made a sound in his throat that she couldn't interpret.

A moment later, he was easing the Prius around and over the potholes and pulled up as close to the back door of the house as he could get. Faith had arrived ahead of them, and together they helped Charlotte from the car.

Her head swam again, and she came close to crumpling against Gray. With a wordless exclamation, he swung her up into his arms.

Charlotte clutched at him and squeaked a protest he ignored. Carrying her effortlessly, he strode up the back steps and through the door Faith held open, then upstairs.

"Which is your room?" he asked.

Cheek against his shoulder, she told him, "First on the left," and tried to remember how much of a mess she'd left it. Faith had always been the neat one, while Charlotte was more inclined to drop her clothes where she shed them.

But she had done a load of laundry yesterday, so it couldn't be too bad, she decided. And he'd hardly expect her bed to be made.

He laid her down as gently as he'd settled her into the Prius. His hands, she thought, lingered a little before he withdrew them. Still bent over, he touched his lips to hers, whispered, "I'll be back in a few hours, Charlotte. Don't you dare go farther than the bathroom," and left after a few quiet words with Faith.

Faith turned on the fan to stir the warm air and kissed Charlotte's cheek.

She tumbled, only a little disorientingly, into sleep again.

"I RECOMMEND A SEMIAUTOMATIC," the gun dealer told Faith, reaching beneath the glass case for a horrifyingly lethal handgun. "Revolvers have some advantages, but generally they're too big for a woman's hand, and it takes too much force to pull the trigger. Now, a .38 like this with a short barrel..." He handed it over the counter to her, grip first.

She'd already told him she had never shot a gun in her life, so he didn't do more than wince when she took hold of the awful thing as if it were a bundle of nettles.

He selected a magazine, took the gun back and inserted it, then reached for earmuffs. "I want you to try half a dozen different guns, pick the one that's most comfortable for you."

Comfortable, she thought semihysterically. She could pretty well guarantee that no matter how much time she put in on the practice range, she was never going to be comfortable with a deadly weapon or with the idea of using it.

She steeled herself by remembering the sight of Charlotte clinging to the door frame, her shoulder blood-soaked and her face grotesquely swollen.

Seeing Charlotte hurt was much worse than remembering her own broken bones at Rory's hands.

Never again, she had vowed, and she'd meant it.

The owner of the gun shop in Everett had been very nice when she explained her needs. He'd had her fill out an application and explained that there would be a 24-hour period before she'd be approved and would be able to buy a gun. Then he'd talked about which weapons he recommended for women and why. Accuracy wasn't her first priority, he'd told her; if she was ever to actually fire the weapon at a human being, it would be at close range. And the standard longer barrel that provided greater accuracy was actually a disadvantage in close quarters. It was easier for the assailant to grab or knock aside, harder for her to lift and aim.

She shuddered at the idea of Rory wrenching a gun from her hand while she hesitated. Any hesitation this time, she knew, could be fatal. His attacks were escalating. He had almost killed her that last time he'd beaten her, before she'd ended her marriage. If he broke into the house again, he surely would.

Charlotte, Faith knew, wouldn't stay. How could she? And Dad would want to defend her, but she hated the idea of him being hurt on her behalf. That was one reason she'd never told her family that Rory was hurting her—she'd known what Dad would do.

The practice range was in the same building, visible through large windows from the shop area.

The owner walked her in and set her up in one of the lanes, showing her how to adjust the target distance and how to hold the gun.

The earmuffs on, both hands gripping the snub-nosed Colt .38, Faith lifted it and aimed at the human-shaped paper target. Her hands trembled. She closed her eyes, breathed slowly and steadied her hands.

This will make us safer. Sometimes the scary choice is the best one.

She pulled the trigger, and lurched back as the gun kicked.

But when, swallowing, she stared at the paper target, she saw the hole through the head.

Now it was her stomach that lurched.

"I don't know if I can do this," she said shakily.

"That was a great start," the gun-shop owner told her. "You get used to the kick. Were you aiming at the torso?"

"That's what you told me to do." He had convinced her that she'd never be a good enough shot to go for the leg or try to wing someone. The torso was the biggest target, and the likeliest to drop the assailant, which was her goal.

He stood behind her and steadied her hands as she fired, and fired again.

Eventually he had her try several different guns. A couple of guys there to practice shoot became interested in her first lesson and began to give advice. She learned that they were Everett police officers. They showed her how to curl her thumb rather than wrap it over her other hand, got her to loosen her grip.

"No tighter than a handshake," one of them said.

She shot until locking her wrists and elbows was becoming automatic, until she could replace the magazines without fumbling, until she was ripping the center out of the paper target.

They were so nice that she began to relax. She had told them tensely why she was buying a gun, and they took her seriously.

She finally chose the very first gun she'd fired, which earned her nods of approval all around. Hugely relieved to take off the earmuffs and hand back the Colt .38 she'd chosen, Faith discovered her knees were weak and that she felt so tremulous her teeth wanted to chatter. She clenched them together, offered her credit card and signed the slip at the bottom.

"I'll be back tomorrow," she told all three men.

"And every day, if I can manage it, until school starts."

"School?" the older cop asked.

"I teach kindergarten."

None of them said a word. They didn't have to. The dichotomy—she thought that was the right word—between who she was and her very presence here, at a gun range, was so vast, so absurd, there really wasn't anything *to* say.

It was Rory's fault. Except…she still couldn't absolve herself for all of it. The blindness that had let her love a man so insecure, so angry. The timidity, the need to be loved, that had kept her silent and meek when he hit her, over and over.

No matter what other people said, including Gray and Ben Wheeler, she couldn't shove all the blame onto Rory. If she'd insisted on counseling the first time he hit her… If she'd left him the second time… It might have been different. Maybe he'd have gotten help. Maybe his rage wouldn't have built and built and built until he hated her for what he'd become.

"Thank you," she said to all three men. "Thank you so much." She turned and fled to her car, where she could sit until she quit shaking. Where she could, in the quiet of her own mind, shore up her resolve.

She stared, eyes dry and burning, at the blank cinder-block wall of the gun range.

If I have to, I'll shoot Rory. If he makes it impossible for me to do anything else.

But the pain balled in her chest told her that if she killed him, the guilt she carried now for her part in the fiasco of her marriage would be *nothing* in comparison.

Taking the life of the man she'd once loved would be so terrible, Faith couldn't imagine ever putting it behind her.

She gripped the steering wheel and prayed, as she'd never prayed before, that this time, Rory had shocked even himself by what he'd done. What he'd *wanted* to do. That he would leave the area, and let go of whatever horrible tie she had on him.

She prayed she would never see him again, that the handgun she'd purchased today would never be fired outside the range and would eventually gather dust in a box in the closet.

But as far as she could tell, none of her prayers where Rory was concerned had ever been heard.

CHAPTER TEN

"NO, WE'RE NOT HAVING DINNER in West Fork." Gray buckled his seat belt and put the key in the ignition. "I can't go anywhere in town without running into a city council member or having half a dozen worthy citizens stop by my table to tell me what I should be doing differently. I figure Everett is safe. Odds are good of going unrecognized."

Charlotte laughed at his pained tone, even though she was ridiculously nervous.

So what if she was having dinner with him? It's not as if she never dated.

But Gray...wow. She'd have chickened out if she could have reconciled it with her conscience. Since she couldn't, here she was sitting in Gray's Prius wearing a pale blue dress with spaghetti straps that she'd borrowed from Faith. And open-toed, strappy heels, also borrowed, because otherwise all she'd brought were flip-flops and a pair of athletic shoes. She'd bothered with earrings for the first time since she got here, and even some makeup.

Gray had been about one thousand times nicer to her than she'd deserved while she was in the hospital, and the past four days, too. When he'd come tearing into the E.R. cubicle, she had been astonished to realize how desperately she had wanted him. Not Dad, not Faith. *Gray.* And there he was.

Having him stay the night, hold her hand, massage her aching head and kiss her more tenderly than anyone had since she was a little girl, all of that meant she owed him. Big-time.

And she hated that she felt so shy and so scared about where this date might go. This man could change her life.

Maybe he already had.

He made the turn out onto the highway, then glanced at her. "How do you feel about Creole food?"

"Is there such a thing around here?"

"Yeah, there's a restaurant called Alligator Soul in Everett. Right on Broadway, so the view is of traffic, not the sun setting over the Sound, but I like the food. If you'd prefer, we could go to Anthony's Homeport down on the marina, or..."

"It so happens, I love eating in New Orleans. I could do nothing *but* eat when I'm there. Who cares about the view?"

Another of his lightning quick assessments

made her even more self-conscious. "You don't look like you do all that much eating."

In other words, he thought she was skinny.

Yes, but he'd been pursuing her single-mindedly since he set eyes on her, so he couldn't mind skinny too much.

Still, her voice was stiff when she said, "I have a good metabolism. Plus, I tend to forget to eat when I'm absorbed in a project."

He didn't say anything for a minute. Conversation, it occurred to her, would be different, since there wasn't anything new to say about Rory. Gray had stopped by the farm several times a day since the assault. Even if he weren't also getting reports from his police chief, he'd have been up-to-date on the search. Which so far was a really embarrassed strikeout. Bases-loaded, bottom-of-the-ninth strikeout. Ben Wheeler was not a happy man. Gray, Charlotte suspected, was even less happy.

He cleared his throat. "Where did you go to college?" He actually sounded interested, though, not as if he were scraping the bottom of the barrel for a conversational ploy.

"University of Chicago. I wanted to try big-city life, preferably far, far from home."

"Why?"

"Why? Don't most small-town kids dream of escape?"

"Your sister went to the U. Forty-five minutes from home."

"Faith and I didn't have much in common." Still didn't, except for a deep panic about Rory Hardesty as well as worry about Dad and what would happen to him if they had to sell the farm.

"You're twins."

"Identical. Gee, tell me about it." The frost in her voice probably wasn't justified, but he'd definitely hit a sore spot. "Which means we should want the same things?"

"Of course not." His fingers flexed on the wheel. "You're right. I shouldn't have said that."

Damn it, that was the trouble with Gray—he was invariably fair-minded, willing to apologize when it was called for, and damn it, he was the only person she ever remembered meeting her and Faith and being surprised they were identical twins.

Uncomfortably, she said, "Faith always knew she wanted to stay in West Fork. She loves kids and wanted to be a teacher from the time she was ten or twelve years old. Me, I was always restless. I wanted to see other places. I knew I didn't want to settle here."

He was quiet for a long time. They'd turned south on I-5. Somehow she wasn't surprised that he drove in the middle lane and never went above the speed limit. She'd have liked to label him stodgy, but couldn't quite make it stick. He was probably careful to be law-abiding because he'd gone into politics. Even a speeding ticket would give an opponent in the next election something to trumpet about. And also, Gray just struck her as a man too confident, too at ease with himself, to need to be aggressive on the road or anywhere else.

Heaven help her, she *liked* that about him.

She liked way too much about him.

And didn't let herself consider why *like* was such an obviously pallid word.

"How did you end up in West Fork?" she asked. "Since you didn't grow up here."

"I chose it. Out of college, I worked at a big firm in Portland. When I decided to strike out on my own, I looked for the right kind of small town. One close enough to a major metropolitan area to make it possible for an architectural firm to succeed, and prosperous enough there'd be at least some business for us right there in town. I wanted someplace I could see myself raising a family."

"You have a traditional view of raising a family?" she asked, knowing she sounded snide but unable to help it. "Kids shouldn't grow up in a city or a busy suburb?"

He shrugged. "Sure they can. That's just not what I want for mine."

There was something more here she didn't get. From what she'd heard, he was not only smart, but also talented. He was sexy, handsome, charming. And he'd *chosen* a life in a backwater town five miles off the freeway, nestled in the foothills of the Cascade Mountains. Not just chosen—he'd entwined himself in West Fork as if determined to be the warp to its weft, or whatever the weaving terms were.

It's true that West Fork had grown a whole lot in the past ten years; several developments had sprung up on the outskirts. But her impression was that most of the newcomers commuted to the city for jobs. They worked at Boeing in Everett, Microsoft in Redmond, or they endured the daily commute into downtown Seattle. They lived in West Fork because they could afford more house here for less money, or because they might be able to own acreage, which they wouldn't be able to do in Seattle or its environs. Yes, their kids went to school here; they might even grocery shop here or use the library. But most of them probably didn't take the local weekly newspaper, pay attention to local politics or care enough to get involved in civic activities. Until Gray, the mayor of West Fork had always been an old-timer. Someone whose roots were here.

What she wanted to know was why Gray Van Dusen had chosen to transplant his roots to this small town.

They arrived at the restaurant, so she shelved her curiosity for now.

When they walked in, everyone who saw her looked at her face, then averted their eyes. She saw some of those glances sneak back, somewhat narrowed, to study Gray.

Once they were seated, he ordered crawfish beignets to start, and seafood jambalaya, while she went for pepper shrimp as an appetizer and the pecan crusted snapper as a main, and had her eye on the sweet-potato pecan pie for dessert. Assuming she hadn't filled up by then, which she thought unlikely.

She grinned at him as the waiter walked away and said, "You know everyone here thinks you're responsible for this face."

He grimaced. "I suppose they do. Nice thought."

"I told you I shouldn't be displayed in public for a while yet." She touched her cheek, which felt better but had become increasingly colorful. Thank goodness, she could open her eye now, but the raccoon black surrounding it was a nice effect coupled with the purple and yellow hues on her temple and cheek.

"I didn't want you to have time to shore up your original resolve to have nothing to do with me."

"I wouldn't have done that." Though if she were absolutely honest with herself, Charlotte wasn't positive that, given a few more days, she might not have figured out a graceful way to say, *I think I'm in love with you but I'm scared of what that means, so let's just not do this, okay?*

"Good," he said softly. "I also figure I have a limited window of opportunity, and I didn't want to lose any days."

She set down her water glass with an audible clunk. "A limited window of opportunity for *what?*"

"To get to know you." He paused, his gaze on her face. "To seduce you." He seemed about to say something else, but thought better of it.

Pure heat flooded her, pooling low in her abdomen. Shocked by her response, Charlotte could only swallow and stare helplessly back at him. *This* was why going out with him, spending time alone with him, was so dangerous.

It took her an embarrassing length of time to produce any kind of respectable comeback. "Well, you're not very confident then, are you?"

His eyes narrowed. "What's that supposed to mean?"

"How many weeks do you figure it'll take

before I succumb?" She might have been having fun, if only she weren't so aroused just because he'd said *to seduce you.*

"I don't know, Charlotte. Why don't you tell me?"

The waiter showed up with their appetizers and drinks. Charlotte smiled and thanked him. Gray didn't even acknowledge the guy's existence, he was staring so hard at her.

"Maybe I can't be seduced," she suggested, reaching for a shrimp.

He reached over the table and gripped her wrist, where her pulse was racing. "And maybe you can."

"Hard to say yet," she said, smiling at him. "I'll give some thought to it."

"You do that." His voice had an unfamiliar note: rough, even jagged, as if he were angry or… She didn't know. He wasn't flirting any more, that was for sure. He hadn't taken that byplay anywhere near as lightly as she would have liked.

She pretended to savor the shrimp, although she didn't taste it at all. Only after a sip of wine did she ask, "Where did you grow up, Gray?"

"Silverton, south of Portland." He began to eat, too. "Until I was eleven, when my parents split up. I bounced between them after that. Mom was in Portland, Dad in Boise."

So the explanation was that simple. In West

Fork, he was trying to recapture something he'd lost when his family fractured.

"I have good memories," he added after a minute. "And I haven't regretted my decision to move to West Fork."

Charlotte only nodded. Weirdly enough, she had a lump in her throat from that small glimpse he'd given her of the hurt boy he'd been after his parents' divorce.

"Were you, um, engaged or something when you settled here?" Oh, Lord. He might even have been married, she realized, not liking how bothered she was by that idea. "Since you were thinking about where you wanted to raise a family."

"No, I just wanted to find the place. I figured marriage and kids would come along eventually."

"But they haven't." She almost whispered it, as if she were intruding somehow.

"No," he said again. The gray of his eyes seemed darker now, and he never looked away from her. "It had to be the right woman."

She felt raw inside, as if she'd just discovered some internal injuries. The idea of him waiting… The memory of how arrested his expression had been that first day, in the barn… Of the way he'd kissed her in the hospital, his shaken voice when he'd murmured, "Ah, Charlotte. I was so scared last night."

Was *she* the right woman, in his eyes? *How could that be?* she wondered in panic. Love at first sight didn't exist. She'd swear it didn't! But, oh, she'd felt something, too, that had grown despite her best efforts to suppress it. She felt a burning under her rib cage at the very *idea* of him being in love with her.

She took a reckless gulp of wine and made herself look around the restaurant, study the band that was setting up in back as if she was the slightest bit interested.

She was being foolish. He hadn't said anything to suggest he wanted more from her than sex.

Then again, there *was* the terror she'd seen in his eyes when he tore into the emergency room, not to mention his tender care when he insisted on staying at her side.

But this could all be explained by his oversize sense of responsibility for his town and its citizens.

"I'd give a whole lot more than a penny for your thoughts right now," he commented.

Charlotte said the first thing that came into her head. "Just…um, looking at all the couples here and wondering if any of them are like Faith and Rory. If what happens at home is a deep, dark secret."

He gave a half laugh. "Another heartwarming thought."

"I'm sorry. Apparently I stink at casual conversation."

"No, you don't. We just haven't tried it yet."

And so they did. Movies, books, music and theater took them through dinner and dessert, national politics through coffee they savored until only a few diners were left in the restaurant. They argued, they laughed and they agreed more often than Charlotte would have anticipated.

After Gray had paid, he took her hand in his as they walked out to the car. It was funny how intimate that felt, more so in a way than having his arm around her. They were palm-to-palm, fingers slotted together. As he released her hand at the car, his thumb traced a leisurely line over her palm. A shiver traveled up her spine.

"Cold?" he asked, voice low and husky.

"No. Just, um…" She couldn't think of any excuse. Not one.

He smiled and went around to his side of the car.

On the drive home he told her about his house, which he'd designed himself. "I served as contractor, too. Gave me a chance to get to know some local tradesmen. The guy who did the woodwork and cabinets is amazing. Likes working by himself, concentrating on one job at a time. The bigger builders need mass-produced material, of course, but I've recommended him for a number of houses I designed."

It didn't take much to get him talking about the process of creation, from first idea through refinement, the consideration of practicalities, and eventually the delicate, detailed work of producing blueprints. Not many people loved what they did, but he was one of them. He liked dreaming, he liked drawing, he reveled in challenges and overcoming obstacles, he was happy out on a work site ankle-deep in mud, smelling the sharp scent of fresh-sawn wood, hearing the pounding of nails being driven in and seeing the bones of his conception before the flesh was added.

"Why on earth," she asked, "do you waste half your time tangling with grumpy people about sewers or parks or zoning instead?"

He laughed. "Let's not forget my personal favorite, which is the yearly budget debate."

"Why?" she asked again, wishing she could see his face better in the dark car.

"I'm good at it." His shoulders moved in an easy shrug. "And I made the decision to invest myself in this town. What I do isn't that different from renovating a house. Taking from this space to make that one more functional, opening up the living area with vaulted ceilings and windows, planning so the cook takes fewer steps, the kids will be playing somewhere Mom can keep an eye on them, allowing for entertainment and privacy and personal quirks. When I build a house, there's constant push and pull, too, you know. The couple who hired me, the contractor, agents for the county, subcontractor. Grandma who stopped by this weekend and really thinks the kitchen should be bigger and that wall should be pushed out and why isn't the laundry room here instead of there. I like people."

"You're very good at…soothing." Sometimes that bothered her, when she felt as though he was manipulating her. Other times… Other times, he made her want to lean on him, burrow in, let his slow, calm voice work on her nerves like a warm bath.

"Am I?"

"You know you are."

She felt prickly now, because they would be arriving at the farm in just a minute. His good-night kiss was unlikely to be gentle and undemanding, not now that he'd confessed to having seduction in mind. Charlotte *wanted* him to kiss her. She'd been thinking about it ever since he'd picked her up, wondering whether it would be slow and honeyed and subversive, or whether he'd used up those tactics and would move on now to open desire. She didn't like the idea that he would stay in control, that this was a campaign. Would she be able to resist either way?

The turn signal went on. Click, click, click. He slowed, eased onto the hard-packed dirt, over the bumps. The sodium lamp near the barn let her see Gray in profile for a moment, although she fixated on his hands, held loosely around the steering wheel. Big, strong, gentle hands.

Nerves quivered in her belly.

It became darker again once the bulk of the barn was between them and the sodium lamp. The back porch light was on, but didn't reach the car. The Prius's headlights swept over the yard and an outlying shed, Faith's Blazer, Dad's pickup. Then Gray pulled in next to the Blazer, set the emergency brake and turned off the lights and the engine.

In the new silence, neither of them moved for a moment.

"I enjoyed myself tonight," he said finally. "I hope you did, too."

She was past lying to him. "I did. I never doubted I would."

He shifted in his seat so he was facing her. "That's why you said no, isn't it?"

"Yes. If—when—I go home to San Francisco, I don't want to have any regrets."

"Too late," he said, an edge in his voice. "Much too late, Charlotte."

He was right. If not for Rory, she could have avoided Gray and saved herself from getting so damn attached to a man who wouldn't settle for a casual relationship. But she hadn't been able to avoid him, and now she felt too much.

He unclicked his seat belt, then hers. His right hand slid under her hair to cradle the back of her head, to hold her still when he bent to capture her mouth.

The kiss wasn't tender, not this time. His mouth demanded that she part her lips, which she did. His tongue stroked hers, and she lost all power to think for perhaps the first time in her life.

A moan vibrated her throat and she reached out to grab him. He angled his head and deepened the kiss. It was hungry, primal…thrust and counterthrust. He tried to haul her against him, to hell with the gearshift, and she would have gone if she could. She had never felt like this, never wanted so much.

He broke the kiss to move his lips over her jaw, to nip her earlobe. He nuzzled her neck, sucked at a sensitive point at the juncture with her shoulder, licked the hollow at the base of her throat. Charlotte distantly heard herself whimper. His hand found her small breasts, shifted from one to the other, rubbing, squeezing her nipples, before he dove back into another long, deep kiss that made her feel boneless and brainless and needy.

She was shaking by the time he went still for what had to be ten seconds. His tongue swept her mouth one more time, slowly, as if to take her taste with him. His lips softened, brushing hers. The hand on her breast became gentle, although he seemed not to want to take it away.

Finally, he nipped her bottom lip sharply enough to make her jump, and lifted his head.

"Unless you want to come home with me…"

She did, of course. So badly that she ached. But panic was going off in her like Fourth of July sparklers. If one kiss could devastate her like this, what would be left of her resolve and independence if she made love with Gray? Would she be *able* to leave if she ultimately decided that's what she ought to do?

She had to think. Weigh what she suspected he was offering against all the rest of her life.

"No," she managed to say, a little shocked that she could still lie to Gray. "Much as I enjoyed that."

"Enjoyed?" He straightened away from her. "I'd have put it stronger than that."

Charlotte felt way too vulnerable to admit that she felt the same. Without saying anything, she opened the car door and got out. She wasn't surprised when she heard his opening, too, or when he met her near the front bumper.

Once again he took her hand, and she realized how damn erotic it could be to lock fingers with someone.

"I can't see any stars," she said.

"Don't you feel how much cooler it's gotten? A cloud cover has moved in. We might have rain tomorrow."

"I think I'll come out and stand in it."

His chuckle felt like another caress. They'd reached the foot of the back steps. Charlotte took out her key. "Thank you for a nice night, Gray."

"You're very welcome." His voice was low and husky. He bent his head and kissed her again, lightly, with the tenderness that had been missing before.

She felt a spurt of fear, or anger, or something. Was that part of his campaign, calculated to weaken her?

Or—God—was he in love with her?

Somehow she made herself turn away, open the screen and unlock the back door. She said good-night, and closed him outside.

As quietly as she'd entered, Dad called, "That you, Charlotte?" from the living room.

"It's me, Dad. I've locked up." She heard the slam of the car door outside, looked out the window to see the headlights come on.

"Faith made a lemon-meringue pie tonight, if you're hungry."

"I've already had pecan pie."

He laughed, a comfortable sound in the dark

house that reminded her a little of Gray's laugh. Her father, before Mom died, had always been at ease with himself, too. No apologies, no sense that he felt he should have made more of his life or regretted roads not taken.

They said their good-nights, and she went upstairs bemused by the realization that her father embodied qualities that drew her to another man.

Gray. What would it have been like to go home with Gray tonight?

THE MORNING AFTER CHAR'S DATE with Gray, Faith was at the range. She hadn't yet put on the earmuffs when she felt the fine hairs on the back of her neck stir. She turned and was curiously unsurprised to find Ben Wheeler standing behind her. He wore jeans today and a T-shirt, both faded and comfortable, molded to his powerful body. His badge was clipped to his belt and he wore his gun in a holster at his hip.

He looked at her with those dark, unreadable eyes. "Leonard tells me you're a hell of a shot."

Leonard was the gunshop and range owner. This was Faith's third visit. She was determined to practice as much as she could before Labor Day and the start of school.

"He's been very helpful."

"I'd have helped if you asked."

"I didn't see any need to bother you," she said coolly. "As you can see, I took your advice, and I'm doing fine."

His expression didn't change much, but she could tell he was irritated. He held out a hand. "Let's see what you got there."

She let him take the .38. He examined it briefly, slid out the magazine, popped it back in, then returned the gun to her.

"Good choice."

"I'm glad you approve. Now if you don't mind..." She nodded toward the target.

A flicker of frustration showed in his eyes, but all he did was nod. "Let's see what you can do."

Her heart was pounding. She hated whatever game he was playing, treating her one minute as if she was precious to him, then walking away the next. She could protect herself and her family. She didn't need Ben Wheeler to give her his approval, or anything else.

But, damn it, her hands were shaking just because he was standing not two feet behind her.

She closed her eyes, breathed slow and deep, and thought, *He doesn't want me. Get over it.* This *is what counts.*

She lifted the Colt, steadied her grip and began firing. By the time she lowered the handgun, the torso of the paper target had been shredded, and a cold stillness had crept over her. Her heartbeat had slowed, and she never turned to look at Ben.

Nor did he say a word.

She knew when he walked away and took up a stance several slots away from hers. He lifted his much larger gun and started firing. *Bang, bang, bang.*

Faith reeled in her target, replaced it with a fresh one and reeled it back out again, farther this time.

That chill still gripped her when she pulled the trigger again.

CHAPTER ELEVEN

DISCREET GOLD LETTERING ON THE glass panel of the door said Van Dusen & Cullen, Architects. The name was also gilded on the sign outside the brick building, shared with a CPA and an attorney.

Gray had asked Charlotte on an afternoon outing. He was going to give her a tour of some of the houses and buildings he had designed, culminating in a picnic at the river.

"But your partner designed the office? Not you?" Charlotte asked, as he ushered her inside.

"Right," he agreed. "Moira is better at something like this."

"What do you mean, 'something like this'?"

"Elegant, straight-forward, possibly stark. Emphasis on function," he explained.

By the time the door was half-open, Moira had spun on her tall stool in front of a slanted drawing table. Like him, she often stood to draw, but this time she was perched, one foot on the floor, the other hooked on the rung of the stool.

"Put-downs," she sighed, clearly having heard him. "Nothing but put-downs." She grinned at Charlotte. "He has no respect for me at all."

Charlotte laughed. "Do you have any for him?"

"Not a bit."

They smiled at each other, and Gray took a moment just to look at them, two women he loved, if in different ways.

Moira Cullen was around Charlotte's height, but voluptuous rather than slender. She was constantly battling with the pounds that her body would have loved to pack on. He'd never quite convinced her that most men preferred generous curves. Moira had brown eyes, copper-red hair and freckles that she detested. Gray and she had flirted the first couple of weeks of their freshman year in college. The next thing they knew, they were friends, both dating other people. Their friendship had endured long after any of the college romances.

Next to her, Charlotte was boyishly slim with small breasts and narrow hips. He could hardly wait to hear Moira grumble about him falling for a woman with the kind of body she envied.

As she chatted with his partner, Charlotte prowled the office, studying the framed architectural drawings hung on white walls. She'd regained all of her intensity since that night in the hospital, he realized. In contrast, Moira was tranquil.

But then, Gray thought with amusement, compared to Charlotte, most people were models of serenity. He almost laughed, thinking of the jolt he felt every time he touched Charlotte. Who would have guessed that his idea of a good time would turn out to be the equivalent of sticking his finger in an electric socket?

Still lounging in the doorway, Gray tuned back in to hear Moira telling Charlotte about how they'd become friends, staying in touch when they took jobs at different architectural firms after college.

"I went home to Missoula," she said. "But we'd always talked about setting up shop together someday, and when Gray told me he'd found the perfect town, I came and checked it out."

"The perfect town," Charlotte repeated, sounding…odd.

"It's beautiful here! Great climate, except in August." She grimaced. With her redhead's skin that was incapable of tanning, Moira hated the relentless sun of August. "Friendly people, easy drive to Seattle for concerts or to see indie films or eat Ethiopian food. What's not to like?"

Charlotte gave her head a shake, as if to clear it. "I grew up here. It looks different to me."

"In what way?" Moira sounded genuinely curious.

Gray waited for Charlotte's answer with even more curiosity. He knew she rarely came home for more than a week a year. Why did she hate West Fork so much?

She glanced at him, but her gaze immediately skittered away. "When I was in high school, I would have told you West Fork was redneck and incredibly boring. Hardly a business in town stayed open past five o'clock, and the restaurants closed at nine." Her prowling had became restless, Gray noticed; she ran her fingers over the glossy chestnut window frame, touched the detailed model of a Frank Lloyd Wright house that sat on his desk, stroked the rim of a cherry wood inbox on Moira's desk. "When the farmers sprayed manure on their fields, it stunk for miles around. The single screen movie theater got pictures weeks after their release dates. The big excitement for teenagers was jumping off the railroad bridge into the river or getting drunk. Every weekend there were keggers. It seemed like nothing around here ever changed." She came to a stop in front of a drawing Gray had done of his own house, low and sprawling with multi-layered decks to take advantage of the river bluff setting.

Even Moira remained silent, watching Charlotte

as though trying to puzzle her out. Gray stayed where he was, tension infusing his entire body. Did her resistance to him come down to this, her dislike of small town living? If so, what was he going to do about it?

But she said, on a sigh, "Of course, I was wrong. West Fork *has* changed. Who'd have thunk?"

"The restaurants don't shut their doors until ten now," Moira agreed.

Charlotte laughed, the sound brittle, but a laugh was a laugh. "No more stench of manure, either. This isn't a farming town anymore. I'm amazed to find that makes me feel sad. I keep thinking about my parents' friends, and realizing how many of them have sold out. The few left are dinosaurs."

Gray stirred. "Kids still jump off that damn railroad bridge, despite our best efforts to stop them."

"I noticed the chain-link along the sides." She shot him a look of mischief. "That's been tried before, you know."

"So I'm told. It deters some."

"It didn't deter me."

He groaned. "Why am I not surprised?"

"Faith would never jump off the bridge," she mused. "I thought she was a wimp."

"It's dangerous." His voice roughened. "A

sixteen-year-old broke his back last summer when he hit a rock. He's paralyzed."

Her eyes widened, the blue so intense he couldn't look away. "Really? I didn't hear. That's awful."

"Preventable."

She blinked. "I can't go back in time and *not* jump."

"Yeah, I know." Gray moved his shoulders. Damn it, what was wrong with him? "The thing that maddens me is that the teenagers are back this summer. They've already forgotten."

"Teenagers do that."

She was right, but he couldn't understand the foolishness. Or maybe it was the callousness than bothered him.

He'd tried to tell himself it was different when you lost a brother rather than a friend. Someone you loved, not just a familiar face from school. Maybe to the local kids, Jason Southard's disappearance from their lives wasn't any different than if he and his family had moved away. Not many of them had been there the day Jason was pulled from the river. Not many of them had visited him in the hospital.

Charlotte was watching him, and he knew that now he'd made her curious. He would tell her about Gerrit, but not yet. A part of him was glad he hadn't. He wanted to understand better what lay between her and Faith first.

Shoving his hands in his pockets, he walked toward Charlotte. "That's my house you were looking at."

"Really?" She turned back and studied it. "It's not the typical Northwest look."

"No, I wanted a lower profile. I liked the idea that you could stand on the riverbank, look up and not even notice the house on the bluff because it belongs there. We're too fond of wanting to dominate nature."

Charlotte was back to looking at him, her mouth curving. "How funny," she said. "When we were driving to Everett, I was thinking that you drive like someone who doesn't have any need to assert himself. You're not very competitive, are you?"

He raised his brows. "Sometimes. I did run for political office and beat the crap out of Tom Hicks."

Her smile widened. "So you did."

"Gray has a way of winning without displays of male dominance," Moira said. "That makes him unusual."

"And sneaky," Charlotte remarked. "He murmurs soft words, and the next thing you know you've agreed to do something you had no intention at all of doing."

Moira chuckled in delight. "Yes!"

Gray glowered at both women. "You mean, I'm polite and reasonable."

"You *disguise* yourself as polite and reasonable." Charlotte looked pleased to have annoyed him. "Really, you're pushy."

Moira was all but falling off her stool now, she was laughing so hard.

Gray eventually dragged Charlotte away, but not until she and Moira had bonded enough to disconcert him. Damn it, maybe they were more alike than he'd thought.

He felt guilty leaving Moira to work. God knows, she was already doing far more than her share since he'd taken office. Now, these past weeks since Charlotte had walked into his life, he was accomplishing even less. Moira claimed not to mind; her income had climbed substantially now that she was handling the majority of the jobs, and they'd talked before he ran for mayor about the resultant stresses.

None of that kept him from feeling guilty.

As he drove by the first of two buildings downtown for which he'd drawn the plans, Gray was discomfited to discover that he was nervous about Charlotte's reaction. She'd clung to his hand in the hospital. She'd responded to his kisses. Otherwise, he didn't know what she thought about him. One of the ways he defined himself was by his work.

But when he pointed out the new Bank of America, she leaned forward and stared, craning her neck to keep looking after the car had passed it.

When she straightened in her seat, she turned to scrutinize him. "I noticed it the first time I came into town. It looks like it might have been here since the 1920s. For a second, I thought, 'Wait, was that here and I've just forgotten it?' But then it's somehow modern, too, and a little bit surprising. How did you do that?"

In partial answer, he pointed out what was wrong with the relatively new bank building just down the block that made it so jarring on the old-fashioned main street where many of the stores still had the false fronts of a classic Western town.

The library was the other building he took pride in, and again Charlotte bathed him in praise. He felt ridiculous for needing her admiration, and embarrassingly grateful she was giving it so generously.

He took her by a couple of houses he'd designed, too, before driving to the small riverside park. There, mothers were pushing kids on the swings or running to keep the merry-go-round spinning. Older kids splashed in the river. No teenagers, thank God, were edging out onto the railroad bridge.

Charlotte and he sat on a park bench above the gravel beach. He set down the cooler that held their lunch and opened it.

He scanned the river, his gaze pausing on a pair of toddlers splashing in a two-inch pool, older kids shrieking and hitting a beach ball back and forth.

"I hope the water was higher when you jumped," he said.

Charlotte had put on dark glasses when they got out of the car, hiding her blue eyes. Her gaze followed his. "I'm sure it was. That pool under the bridge doesn't look very deep right now."

"It's not. I haven't been for a swim in a while, but I've never noticed that boulder sticking above the water." He pointed to a spot in the shadow of the bridge.

"I don't remember it, either, and Faith and I used to spend hours and hours here every summer. She said there was something of a drought this winter, so I suppose there wasn't much snowmelt."

He nodded, and told her about problems people with shallow wells were already having. Those on city water were okay, but were being encouraged to conserve.

"You know," he said, handing her a sandwich

and a bottle of water, "you've never told me much about what you do for a living. What kind of software were you working on?"

She unwrapped the sandwich and lifted the focaccia bread to inspect its innards.

"Turkey and pepper-jack cheese," Gray said. "And some kind of chipotle sauce. Spicy."

The sandwiches were stuffed with vegetables, too. "Yum," she said, and took a bite.

Gray enjoyed watching her. Sitting here in the sun on a day cooler than any in the past month, she appeared remarkably relaxed, one leg curled under her so she could half-face him. A breeze ruffled her hair, revealing pale gold roots. He played with the image of her blond like her sister. Funny how sure he was that he still wouldn't have any trouble telling them apart. Today she wore the airy skirt she'd had on the first time he saw her, and probably the same top, too, although now her bare arms and legs were golden instead of white. He was pretty sure the flip-flops were the same, too. She had pretty feet, narrow and high-arched, with toenails freshly painted bright coral.

He liked the idea that she'd painted her toenails for his benefit.

Once she'd swallowed, Charlotte said, "Most of my work has been on computer security. The eternal problem. We come up with a solution, hackers find a way around it. Do you know anything about information cards?"

"Actually, yes. I've learned more than I wanted to know when the city upgraded its computers and software this spring. Apparently there had been problems in the past with employees who told their browsers to remember their passwords."

She nodded. "So the next person who sat down at that desk logged on with someone else's name and password, and then you can never tell who did what. Right. Well, we were coming up with new version of the information card that we hoped would be more widely accepted. One of the big benefits would have been making online transactions more secure. It would exchange encrypted data with the bank to authorize the transaction without the purchaser entering a credit card or bank number."

"'Would have been'?"

"OpTech—that's who I worked for—is flirting with bankruptcy. At least half the programmers lost their jobs. We were in a neck-and-neck race with another software company to get a better product on the market, and I'm going to guess they'll win."

"Was it a surprise?" he asked. "Getting laid off?"

She made a face. "Yes. We were so close. I thought any cutbacks would be in another division.

I would have started job-hunting if I'd had any idea."

"Would you have been able to get time off to help out here at home if you hadn't been out of a job?" *Would I have ever met you?* he wondered.

"I don't know." Charlotte gazed out at the river, but not as if she actually saw it. "I didn't really want to come home."

Gray made no effort to fill the silence. Instead, he ate his sandwich, waiting her out, feeling the struggle in her.

"No, of course I would have come," she finally said, her voice filled with new tension. "Dad's accident was bad enough, but then when Faith told me about Rory..." She shuddered. "Imagine if she'd been alone."

The barn would have burned down, no question. Or worse—given the summer-long heatwave and lack of rain, the flames might have leaped to outbuildings, or crawled over dry grass to the house.

And sure as hell, if the conflagration hadn't driven Faith and her father from the farm, she'd have been hurt instead of Charlotte the night Rory broke in. Worse, Gray thought, because she wouldn't have known how to fight back. Had she ever fought back when she was married to the son of a bitch? Gray doubted it. No, Faith had been willing to wield the baseball bat in defense of someone else she loved, but not herself.

After a minute, he said, "You know Faith bought a handgun."

"Boggles the mind," Charlotte murmured. "Yes, I know. She went to the range to practice this morning. She's determined."

"Wheeler saw her there this morning. Says she decimated a target while he was watching. Apparently she's damn good for a beginner."

"Faith." Still incredulous, she shook her head.

"This town's not the only thing that can change."

"People do. I know that." And, clearly, she wasn't happy about it. Her consternation might have amused him if so much hadn't been riding on her willingness to acknowledge that maybe her own desires had metamorphosed, too. "It's not always good, you know," Charlotte grumbled. "Look what happened to Rory. And Dad. He's not the same man he was."

"Isn't he?" Gray asked gently. "A hell of a lot has altered around him. Twenty years ago, if you'd asked him what his life would be like today, I'm betting he'd have told you he'd still be farming the way he always did, he and your mom would be celebrating their…what? Thirtieth anniversary? And his girls would be happily settled in life. Is he really a different man, or the same one reacting to the crap life's thrown at him?"

She was silent for a long time, her face partially averted. "I don't know," she said at last, sounding as if her throat were a little clogged. "He's just so sad."

Gray wadded up his sandwich wrapper and slid closer to her on the bench, laying his arm around her shoulders. "Wouldn't you be?"

Even more quietly, she said, "I am."

"Yeah." The desolation in her voice wrenched something in his chest. "I know you are." He wrapped his other arm around her, too.

Instead of resisting, she turned and leaned into him, her face pressed to his chest.

He just held her, that painful burning inside telling him he'd do damn near anything to ease Charlotte's distress. To make her happy.

This woman and no other.

How the hell had that happened, when she'd given him so little encouragement?

He fought the compulsion to tell her he was in love with her. She wasn't ready to hear those words, and Gray knew she wouldn't be receptive.

What he didn't understand was why she was so resistant to the idea of falling in love.

Or was it that she didn't want to fall in love with him in particular?

Eventually she gave a small sniffle and straightened away from him. He let one arm drop, but kept the other loosely draped around her. He squeezed her upper arm.

"You okay?"

"Yeah." The smile she offered him had a twist to it. "I've spent so little time at home, you know. And now that I'm here, I feel like a stranger in a strange land."

Gray didn't think that was it at all. In fact, his best guess was that she felt just the opposite—she was *too* involved, *too* invested. Charlotte Russell, he believed, was shocked to find out how much she cared about her home and family, and what she'd be willing to sacrifice to keep them safe.

But he didn't argue, because she'd have snapped right back at him. She thrived on argument. Soaked it up like fertilizer spread on the fields.

Shit, in fact, he thought with a certain wryness.

No, he wasn't ready to let her don her prickly armor again. He'd refused to take advantage of her vulnerability after she was hurt, but today was different.

"Why have you been so determined to stay away from home?" he asked.

Her body went rigid. He wasn't surprised when,

after a careful moment, she rose to her feet so that his hand had to drop away.

"It's…complicated," she said.

Gray leaned back against the park bench and studied her. "Too complicated to explain?"

Her hesitation was just long enough for him to suspect she wasn't going to answer at all, or would lie if she did.

But after a minute she said, "I just can't talk about it. I pretty much despise myself these days, and if you don't mind I'd rather not have you becoming the drum major for my parade."

What the hell…?

"Did you kill someone?"

"No." She looked at him without expression, any turbulence in her eyes hidden behind the dark glasses. "I'd better be getting back. I told Faith I'd only be gone a couple of hours."

Gray nodded. "We're only shelving this, you know. I can be patient, but I'm a stubborn man."

Her mouth curved, although he didn't know how amused she actually was. "Gee, you think?"

He gathered up the remains of their lunch and they walked back to the car, side by side but not touching. Conversation was sparse during the drive, too. He pulled up in front of the barn, feeling something close to despair. Was Charlotte going to say goodbye and mean it?

This time, he set the emergency brake but didn't turn off the ignition. Charlotte unfastened her seat belt, but then didn't move for a minute, as if she were gathering herself.

"Would you like to come to dinner?" she asked, the words hurried. "Probably not tonight, we'll be having leftovers. But maybe tomorrow? Of course, we eat with our plates on our laps to keep Dad company in the living room, but..."

Relief hammered him. "Yes," he said. "I'd like that. Tomorrow works."

"Oh." Charlotte swallowed and turned her head. "I'm sorry to be so difficult. I've been kind of a mess lately."

"Not a surprise, considering you lost your job, came close to losing your father and have been fighting tooth and nail to keep your sister safe and the farm going."

"Well...I suppose not." Her smile was only semisuccessful. "I actually had a lovely time today, until..."

"We got too serious."

"I keep dumping on you." Quickly, taking him by surprise, she leaned toward him and kissed his cheek.

Gray turned his head, caught the back of her head and made the kiss serious, too. It didn't last long, but had his heart feeling like a Frisbee at the highest point in its arc.

When he let her go, he saw that she was as shaken as he felt.

"Tomorrow," he said roughly.

She nodded, got out of the car, and said, "Goodbye," before slamming the door and hurrying into the barn, her skirt swirling around her long slender legs.

Gray didn't put the car in gear for a long time.

She had kissed him. She'd asked him to dinner. It was the first time Charlotte had reached out to him, and that gave him hope.

And damn, he thought, hope hurt almost as much as falling in love.

CHAPTER TWELVE

GRAY CAME TO DINNER, and was an agreeable guest who spent as much time entertaining and charming Faith and Dad as he did Charlotte. Not that she ever relaxed, even for a minute. Even when he was answering a question Faith had asked, or telling a story for Dad's benefit, he had a way of glancing at Charlotte, just letting his gaze rest on her for a moment, that had darn near the same effect on her his kisses did. There was heat in his eyes when he looked at her, coupled with something speculative that alarmed her almost as much.

Later that week, he came by and brought lunch, catching Charlotte alone. Faith had talked over dinner about how she had to spend time getting her classroom ready and attending an in-service training day. Apparently Gray had an excellent memory.

He happened to arrive when she was waiting on several customers simultaneously. He seemed content to lend a hand, chatting with a young couple checking out the antiques, even ringing up a couple of purchases on the old-fashioned cash register. The two of them barely managed to snatch bites of the quesadillas he'd brought and exchange a few words. Although, damn it, she knew he was watching her.

When she realized he was leaving, Charlotte said, "Excuse me for a moment" to the woman debating which hand-painted sign she wanted, and hurried to catch up with him before he reached his car.

"Gray."

He turned, brows raised. "You didn't have to rush out here. I know you're busy."

"I just wanted to, um, thank you."

Gray took two steps so that he stood right in front of her. So close she could feel his body heat. Then he took her face in both hands, tipped it up and kissed her. A brush of his lips, a slide of his tongue, a graze of teeth. "I just like seeing you," he whispered, and let her go.

She was still standing there when he backed the Prius out, although she thought it was a miracle her legs were supporting her.

Charlotte made herself turn away, not keep gaping like a lovesick teenager until his car was out of sight.

Oh, God. What was she going to do about Gray Van Dusen?

Today, two days later, he showed up again, this time with burgers and fries from Tastee's.

"I brought condiments on the side since I don't know what you like," he announced, raining packets of mustard and ketchup on the countertop beside the drinks and the white paper bags holding the burgers and fries.

There was only one shopper this time, a middle-aged woman who was outside browsing the perennials. She'd told Charlotte earlier that she enjoyed taking her time deciding what she wanted for a new flower bed she had in mind.

Gray leaned one hip against the counter as he took his burger out of the bag, lifted the bun off and squeezed mustard in a spiral atop the lettuce, onions and tomato.

"You'll get that on your tie," Charlotte warned, watching as the mustard oozed out when he picked up the burger.

He glanced down. "Yeah. Damn. I need a bib." Unselfconsciously, he tucked the corner of a paper napkin inside his shirt and patted it over his chest.

"Cute," Charlotte told him, before popping a couple of fries in her mouth.

He must have had meetings this morning, or would this afternoon, because he wore dark slacks, dress shoes, a white shirt and a conservative red-and-gray striped tie. Darn it, she was spending entirely too much time imagining him wearing nothing at all.

Which would mean *she* wasn't wearing any clothes, either. And then he would be touching her, and she'd be touching him. Feeling the leap of his heart under her hand. Finding out whether he had much chest hair, whether his body was as fit as she suspected.

Whether he would like what he saw when he looked at her.

Charlotte's dreams had become unnervingly erotic. She'd been attracted to men before, but never to the point where the attraction bled over into her sleep.

"Eat," he ordered her, "before you get busy again."

"I haven't been busy yet today." She did obediently unwrap her burger. "The other day was an anomaly."

"How goes the maze?"

"Now, *that's* popular. But mostly weekends, when parents are free to bring their kids and when Mr. Barth is over here with one of his Clydesdales and the wagon."

Gray nodded. He knew they were offering free wagon rides, courtesy of a kindly neighbor who was thrilled to have an excuse to show off his prized horses.

"Faith's first day at school is Tuesday." Charlotte

found herself looking at the hamburger in her hand as if she didn't know what it was. "I don't know how long I should stay, Gray. Dad won't really be on his feet for another month. Last year Faith hung a Closed sign on Mondays, hired someone half days to help Dad Tuesday through Friday, then took care of weekends herself. Well, she and Dad did."

Charlotte had the impression that Dad had mostly done the physical labor—tilling fields, planting the corn and pumpkins, pruning berries, watering and hauling and making deliveries when necessary in his beat-up old truck. He was reluctant to operate the cash register at all, Faith had admitted, and wasn't fond of chatting up customers, either.

"I'm not sure how much I'm really needed now, except I keep worrying..."

"About Hardesty."

"Yes."

Gray set down his half-eaten burger. "You should worry about him." His voice was gruff. "I can't believe he's done."

"No, me neither." She looked up unhappily. "But what if he is? I can't put my life on hold forever."

A frown deepened lines on his forehead. "Is that what you think you're doing? Treading water?"

"What would you call it?" she shot back. "I should be job hunting."

"Can't you do that from here?"

She let out a sigh, hoping it would ease the constriction she felt in her chest. He'd taken what she said wrong, Charlotte could tell. He was wondering if she thought *he* was a time filler for her, a diversion while she waited to get back to her real life. She wished that's all he was. Whatever he was doing to her, whatever her sister and her father and her home were doing to her, scared the daylights out of Charlotte. All of this felt so real to her, but was it? Wasn't this exactly what she'd run away from? The farm, the hometown boy, her sister?

"I am," she said. "I've been looking online, that is. I just put my résumé out there. But what if somebody in the Bay Area calls suddenly and wants to interview me?"

He didn't look happy about the idea, but he said, "You fly down there."

"If I had to buy an airline ticket for a next-day flight, it would cost a fortune. And look at me!" She yanked at her hair. "I'd have to get to a salon, and I've got scratches on my arms and my fingernails look like I've been scrabbling in gravel." For some reason, the sight of her hands horrified her, as if their state represented everything that had changed since she'd flown in from

San Francisco, where she'd been living the life she'd chosen.

Gray reached out and caught her hand in his bigger one. He lifted it and pressed his lips to her knuckles. "People garden, or remodel houses. You'll be hired for your skill, not your manicure."

As quickly as she could without being obvious, Charlotte took her hand back. It curled into a fist at her side. She could still feel that gentle pressure on her knuckles.

"Oh, I know. I just feel…unprepared."

He watched her, his eyes grave. "Have you considered looking for a job up here? Surely there are as many opportunities in the software industry in Washington these days as there are in Silicon Valley. And you'd be closer to your dad and sister."

She wasn't ready to tell him that she *had* been concentrating on openings up here. She had to figure out herself what she really wanted first.

"I've thought about it," she admitted, "but I own a condo in San Francisco. I have friends. You know." No friends, she realized, that she had actually missed or even bothered to call in the past month. Which said something about her life in recent years.

The single shopper appeared with a couple of flats of fall-blooming perennials and Charlotte rang up her purchases. A van pulled in then and disgorged a harassed-looking woman and five boys ranging from about six years old to ten or eleven.

Gray said, "I'd better get back to work," kissed her cheek and left. Charlotte took the woman's money and walked the group out to the maze. The boys were whooping and playing an aggressive game of tag that had the youngest one crying before they reached the entrance.

As the boys plunged in ahead of her, the woman muttered, "Maybe if I let them run ahead they'll get lost and it will take them *forever* to find their way out."

Charlotte laughed despite her distress over how she and Gray had parted. "That's a plan."

The other woman sighed and raised her voice, "You wait for me!"

One of the boys danced back into the opening. "Well, then, hurry!"

"Speaking of getting lost..." she said.

"I'll give you half an hour," Charlotte promised. She took a look at her watch. "If you haven't reappeared, I'll come looking for you."

The woman grinned. "Deal. Thanks."

Charlotte stood there for a minute, listening as the voices grew increasingly muffled. She wished Gray was back at the barn, waiting for her.

Except, at the same time, she was glad he'd

left, because he had too many questions for which she didn't have answers. It was hard, losing all the certainties that had been her guideposts. Especially when she was with him, Charlotte felt as if she'd been stranded out in the open after a tornado warning, when the very air prickled with electricity and the hush was absolute and more terrifying than any sound would have been. Back when she lived in the Midwest, she'd once seen a tornado advancing against a sky too dark for midday, had felt the charged air and the danger.

The instinct to run was powerful. *But how,* she wondered miserably, *do I run from myself?*

FRIDAY MORNING WHEN SHE checked her e-mail on her laptop, she had a request for a job interview at a small software company in Redmond. The commute wouldn't be more than forty-five minutes each way from West Fork. She called and set it up for Tuesday afternoon.

Midday, demonstrating the adage that when it rains, it pours, her cell phone rang and she found herself talking to a personnel director at a company called SysPro in San Mateo, part of the Silicon Valley hub south of San Francisco.

"Yes," she said, feeling numb. "I'd love to come in for an interview. Tuesday would be a challenge for me, but… Yes, I can make Thursday this coming week. Yes, thank you."

The numbness was wearing off by the time she ended the call, although she wasn't at all sure what she was left feeling.

She'd have to sell her condo either way; with Bay Area traffic, she'd want to live closer to SysPro if she took a job there.

Maybe she shouldn't go for that interview at all. Except…she shouldn't close doors when she was still in such turmoil. That would be foolish.

Faith arrived home from target practice at the gun range in Everett and had one of the egg-salad sandwiches Charlotte had made for lunch. The part-time employee who helped Faith out during the school year arrived then for a walk-through to see what had changed since spring.

On impulse, Charlotte drew her sister aside. "I've been thinking it would be fun to go for a swim in the river. You know it'll be a madhouse this weekend." It was, after all, Labor Day weekend. "Do you think Marsha would stay for a while so we could go? We haven't had much fun lately," she coaxed.

Seeing the pleasure on her sister's face made Charlotte feel guilty all over again. She'd noticed that Faith had become increasingly withdrawn and even grim. Why hadn't she tried to do more to relieve her sister's mind?

I won't tell her about the job interviews yet. Not today. Maybe we really can just have fun.

Faith nodded. "I'll ask."

Marsha, a round-faced, slightly plump woman not much older than they were, said, "Nobody needs me at home until dinnertime. Go! Take your time."

Charlotte hadn't brought a swimsuit and had to borrow an old one of Faith's.

They certainly weren't alone when they got to the river park, although it would be far more crowded tomorrow. By unspoken consent, they made their careful way over a heap of tumbled boulders upriver, under the railroad bridge. Charlotte had noticed a uniformed police officer talking to a group of teenage boys beside the tracks, presumably having intercepted them before they could scramble up the embankment and onto the bridge. Not Ben Wheeler, thank goodness. Charlotte wasn't quite sure what had happened between Ben and Faith, but whatever it was had played a part in Faith's obvious unhappiness.

Rory. Ben. Me. Gee, I wonder why she's bummed?

"Here," she suggested, and Faith nodded and spread her beach towel in a gravelly cove. A couple of older kids had made their way up and were taking turns jumping off a rock, but otherwise the sisters had this stretch of river to themselves.

Both wore their flip-flops to the water's edge, then gingerly waded in barefoot.

Charlotte winced from the first step. "Wow, I don't remember it being so rocky."

Faith snorted. "You mean, our feet weren't so tender. We went barefoot practically all summer, remember? I always hated having to stuff my feet back into shoes when school started."

"I'd forgotten." Charlotte inched farther out, until the current swirled around her knees. On the plus side, she thought, her feet were now getting numb. "I didn't remember how cold the river was, either."

"Whine, whine, whine. This was your idea."

Charlotte splashed her.

And got splashed back. Water flew back and forth until they were both drenched and laughing, and were able to immerse themselves with only a few muted squeals.

They floated, and took turns with the boys doing cannonballs off the rock. Eventually, they got out and lay on their beach towels, letting the sun bake them.

"You know," Faith said lazily, "this is the first time I've been all summer."

"I'm not surprised." Charlotte rolled over onto her stomach. "You work too hard, Faith."

She braced herself for her twin to take offense, but there was a long silence instead. Then

Faith said, in a low voice, "I don't know what else to do."

"Do you imagine going on like this forever?"

Faith sat up and wrapped her arms around her knees. She looked out at the river rather than at her sister. "I don't think about forever. Just… tomorrow. Next week. Getting by."

"Is that any way to live?"

Faith looked at her. "Do *you* think about forever?"

Now it was Charlotte's turn to hesitate. At last she said, "I suppose lately I have been."

"Because of Gray?"

Reluctantly she nodded.

"Has he told you he's in love with you? Or asked you to stay?"

Charlotte huffed out a breath. "No. But…I think that's what's on his mind. Or maybe I'm imagining it. Maybe *I'm* the one who is starting to think about things like that."

"Are you really?" Faith's voice was almost neutral, but hope, painfully fragile, shone on her face.

Charlotte rolled over again and sat up, too. There would never come a better time to say this. She'd been a coward long enough. "I need to tell you how sorry I am. I don't expect you to understand or to forgive me, but…I want you to know I missed you all the time, even when I couldn't bear to be close to you. I think..." She swallowed. "I think I've been lonely for most of my life. And it was my own fault."

"Why?" her sister asked, in a voice that hurt to hear. "Was it me?"

Charlotte shook her head. Tears ran down her face. She swiped at them, embarrassed. She never cried. "It was always me. But I don't know why. I've never known. It was just...always there, this awful fear clawing at me. I was terrified that I'd somehow be lost if I didn't tear myself away from you."

Faith was crying, too. "Maybe I almost smothered you in the womb."

Charlotte's laugh came out as more like a hiccup. "Maybe." She said tentatively, "I saw a counselor for a while, in Chicago. I didn't get any answers."

Her sister scrubbed both hands over her face. "You've been different since you came home."

"I *feel* different. I don't know why that is, either. Before, I always had this mindset when I was home. I'd practically cross the days off on the calendar."

Faith nodded. "I could tell."

"But this time, I looked at you one day and had no trouble at all distinguishing myself from you.

The ways we're alike aren't much more than skin deep."

Faith's breath hitched. "I've realized something, too."

"What?" Charlotte asked after a minute, when her sister didn't go on.

"It was when I was married, and Rory got so possessive. He didn't want me doing things with friends. He wasn't even happy if I was reading and he was watching TV. I had to be with him, paying attention to whatever he was doing, as if the only way I could prove I loved him was to be one hundred percent focused on him. Even if he'd never hit me, I couldn't have gone on living that way. It was horrible. The harder he grabbed hold, the more I slipped away."

Charlotte nodded, puzzled.

"I think I tried to do that to you. You wanted some space, and that was a threat to me. I was so afraid of being abandoned by you, I tried to grab hold, too."

Even as Charlotte shook her head, a part of her was examining the notion and thinking, *maybe*. If Faith had just taken dance lessons and let Charlotte play soccer instead, if she'd made other friends the way Charlotte had done, things might have been different. But it had seemed like whatever Charlotte did, Faith had to do, too. She and Faith had shared the same social group, and almost all the same classes once they entered the academic track in middle school and high school. Even when they started dating, Faith had always been hungry to hear what Charlotte thought and felt, and to share what *she* felt about the guy she was seeing.

"I always thought," Charlotte said with difficulty, "that *I* was the dysfunctional one. That twins were supposed to *want* to be inseparable. That I was failing you, I suppose."

Faith astonished her by taking her hand. "Well, I've come to believe that it wasn't all you rejecting me. Maybe we could have been good friends and sisters, if only I hadn't been so desperate for more."

"The funny thing is," Charlotte confessed, "this last month I've been realizing how close we actually were. After leaving home, I mostly remembered the struggle inside me, and the way you'd look at me sometimes with such bewilderment and hurt. But lately, little stuff keeps popping into my head. Things that made us laugh, or nights we whispered together until Mom had to yell at us. Playing in the cornfield, dressing up in Grandma Peters's clothes. And I remember what it was like having someone I could absolutely, always, count on."

Faith gave a tremulous smile. "Maybe that's

something that never changed. Because when I really needed you, you came."

Charlotte was a mess, but she didn't care. She could blow her nose when they were done saying important things. "I wish you'd told me sooner that you needed me."

"You mean, when I was married." Faith went quiet for a minute, finally whispering, "I wish I had, too."

"That's bothered me more than anything," Charlotte confessed. "That you didn't feel you could tell me what was happening."

"Maybe if we hadn't had problems I would have. But, well, that's what I wanted to tell you. I think going our own ways was good for both of us, not just you. I screwed up big-time with Rory, but I did leave him. Lately I've realized that I like who I am now a lot better than I did in high school. I used to always see myself through your eyes. Whatever I did or said, I'd sneak a look to see what you thought about it. And that wasn't good."

"'Mirror, mirror, on the wall,'" Charlotte said softly.

Faith sniffed, gulped and nodded. "Exactly. I had to ask the mirror whether I was worthy. And…I always thought the answer was no."

"Because you weren't me. I never should have been your mirror."

"Yes."

"Wow," Charlotte said after a minute. "We really messed up, didn't we?" She was a little shocked to feel a laugh bubbling up through the grief. "I can't tell you how good that felt to say. *We* messed up. Not just me." She flung her arms around her sister. "Even if you made all that up… thank you."

Faith was laughing, too. "I didn't. And I like 'we' too. It sounds way better than 'I'."

"Yes, it does."

"I think," Faith said, "we need to jump back in the river. The cold water will do wonders for puffy eyes."

Charlotte jumped to her feet. "Plus, it feels fabulous."

"Race ya."

Giggling like a pair of teenage girls, they plunged back in.

WHEN HE'D INVITED HER TO DINNER Saturday night, Gray had told Charlotte he wanted to cook for her. He had half expected her to make an excuse. Going to his house where they would be totally alone suggested a next step in their relationship he hadn't been sure she would be willing to make, at least not yet.

If ever.

But she had only asked, after the tiniest of pauses, "*Can* you cook?"

"When you live alone, you either subsist on takeout and microwave dinners or you learn to cook. I get enough fast food for lunch."

What he really wanted was to see her in his house. Find out whether she looked and felt at home there.

The moment he opened the front door and she stepped inside, letting out a wondering sigh, he knew he'd been an idiot even to worry. Of course she belonged here.

"It's beautiful," she murmured, walking straight through from the entry across the living room to the wall of glass that looked out over the river and valley below.

He followed her, his hands in his pockets, and watched as she first drank in the view, then turned and began to explore his house with the same restless curiosity she'd displayed at his office. This level was almost entirely open, living and dining areas and kitchen defined by function but not walls. Only his office and the bathroom on this floor had walls and doors.

She liked to touch—the modern, custom-made dining table, the river stones that made up the massive fireplace, the granite kitchen countertops. She peeked through the small-paned French door into his office, then paused at the top of the staircase that led down.

"Do I get the grand tour?"

"Sure." He strolled over to join her, enjoying the way she caressed the cherry handrail where it curled to an end—like a cat napping in sunlight—atop the newel post, one of the small details he'd designed himself and that gave him pleasure. His fingers knotted into fists. He knew if he didn't keep his hands in his pockets they'd be reaching for her, and it was too soon for that yet.

The bedrooms were downstairs, not directly beneath but rather a step down the bluff, like terraced fields in Italy. The deck off the living room rested atop the bedrooms, which had their own decks. All three rooms had French doors leading outside. His was the largest, with a walk-in closet, sitting area and bathroom with a hot tub and separate shower. As with the upstairs, the floors were bamboo stained the color of cherry. Rugs he'd picked up over the years added warmth and color here and there. The furnishings were still somewhat sparse, because he added pieces when something caught his eye, and lately he'd been too busy to look.

When Charlotte stepped into his bedroom, Gray tensed and stayed behind in the hall.

Not yet.

Her cheeks, he thought, were a little pink when she hastily retreated.

For now, the last bedroom was for guests while the middle one served as his library and held a little-watched television. Two walls had floor-to-ceiling bookcases. The TV and DVD player were on another wall, and the fourth one was made up of windows and a French door. Charlotte walked fully into this room, turning slowly to take in the two oversize leather chairs, the walls of books, and the sunshine falling in through the south-facing windows.

"Gray, your house is perfect."

He'd propped a shoulder against the door frame. "Thank you."

Interestingly, her voice had sounded husky, as if she was fighting off emotion. Gray hoped that was it. He liked thinking that she felt a surge of lust for his house. After all, it was an extension of him, more so than for most people.

"You can wander around some more if you'd like," he suggested. "I'll go get started on dinner."

"Can I help?"

"Nope. It's simple."

She reappeared upstairs when he had the salad put together and the oven heated to broil the steaks that had been marinating all day. Gray wondered if she'd stolen another look into his bedroom, maybe even imagined herself in his bed.

Yeah, he thought, *she would definitely have done that, whether she was working at shoring up her resistance or not.*

And, damn, he'd been half-aroused since he picked her up. He hoped she hadn't noticed.

Charlotte settled on a stool across the counter from him and watched while he put the steaks in to broil and sautéed vegetables.

"I had to rescue a couple from the maze today." Her amusement was plain. "It was awful, because the man was so embarrassed and the woman so relieved. You know how hot it was."

After a week that had been cooler, culminating in a day with gray skies and drizzle, the mercury had shot up again. The bank thermometer had read ninety-eight when he'd driven by at midday.

"They were both red-faced and I was afraid they'd get heatstroke if I left them in there too long. But I could tell I'd undercut his manhood. Never ask directions, you know."

He grinned at her. "That's a stereotype. Some of us do ask directions."

"Mmm-hmm." A smile quivered at the corners of her mouth. "Are you one of them?"

"When necessary." He raised his brows. "Since

I have an excellent sense of direction, it's rarely necessary."

"Sure."

"Who got us out of the corn maze?"

"You did," she admitted.

"I'll bet you know it by heart by now."

"Oh, yeah."

"Does anybody just push their way through the damn corn and force their way out?"

"Not since I've been the gatekeeper. You'd have to ask Faith that."

He'd set two places at the table with woven bamboo place mats and a vase of late summer roses he'd bought from a Vietnamese woman who sometimes sold cut flowers at a corner of the gas-station parking lot. He thought eventually he'd enjoy a perennial bed out front of the house, but he had no time for gardening right now, and was grateful that his master plan hadn't included a lawn that required mowing, fertilizing and aerating.

In unspoken agreement they kept conversation light while they ate. She told a couple more stories about customers and made him laugh at Faith's dread upon finding that the Graves kid—notorious for temper tantrums thrown at the grocery store—had been assigned to her classroom. He talked about the eccentric residents of West Fork who'd made his job as mayor interesting, and sketched on his napkin to show Charlotte his ideas for a house he'd been commissioned to design. He told her that he was making a quick trip to Spokane to talk to the client and walk the site.

"I'm leaving in the morning," he said. "That's one reason I wanted to spend this evening with you. I should be home Tuesday or Wednesday."

She nodded and the conversation moved on before Gray could tell whether she'd miss him at all.

His one near misstep was when he nodded at her hair and asked, "Are you planning to go back to being blond?"

She wrinkled her nose. "I'm ambivalent. Do I want to go with the new me or the old me?"

"Ah," he said softly. "But which color is which?"

Alarm flared on her face. After a minute she said, "That's the question, isn't it?"

He chose to let it go, asking if she'd like regular coffee or iced.

The sun was still well above the horizon when they took their iced coffees out onto the deck. Charlotte, he noted, was looking more skittish now.

Gray let her settle into an Adirondack chair while he remained standing, leaning back against the railing with his ankles crossed. Despite the casual pose, he was watching her closely when he said, "This seems like a good time to talk about why you stayed away from West Fork and never wanted to come back, don't you think, Charlotte?"

She sat in silence for a moment and then said, "Oh, fine. Why not? If I were to stay around, you'd have to know eventually, wouldn't you?"

His heart took a hard thump. It might still be *if,* but she was thinking about staying in West Fork. There was *nothing* she could tell him that would kill the exultation rising in him like a high tide.

"So—" he took a sip of the coffee "—I'm waiting."

CHAPTER THIRTEEN

OH, LORD, CHARLOTTE THOUGHT IN PANIC. How had she let Gray back her into a corner like this? The last thing in the world she wanted to do was admit to him, of all people, how awful she'd been to Faith.

She reminded herself that she might end up going back to California, anyway, coming home to West Fork for only occasional, brief visits in the future. If that was the choice she made, he'd surely start dating another woman, and before she knew it Faith would casually mention that he'd gotten married. Eventually, Faith might even have his children in her kindergarten classroom.

Excruciating jealousy seized Charlotte. She'd never felt anything like it before. Images flipped through her mind: Gray smiling down at that other woman, smoothing her hair back from her face, laughing and hoisting a little boy who looked like a small version of him into his arms…

She'd never given a lot of thought to whether she'd like to have children someday. Perhaps the idea had been too disquieting, given that she preferred not to think about her own childhood. All in all, it was a great time to discover that she *hated* the idea of Gray having kids that weren't hers.

But if she were to stay in West Fork and see what happened with Gray, sooner or later she'd have to tell him how she had felt about Faith, and about being a twin. So it might as well be now. If he despised her when she was done, well, that would help her make up her mind to concentrate on finding a job in the Bay Area and not up here.

To buy herself a moment, she sipped her coffee and let her eyes rest on the green valley below and the bluffs beyond, where large, expensive homes built since she'd left town were half concealed by trees.

She stole a glance at him, and felt an uncomfortable spasm. He was…oh, probably not the handsomest man she'd ever met, but close, with that untidy gold-streaked bronze hair, a face that was pure man and calm gray eyes that suggested not so much an easy temperament as utter control over himself. And those lovely shoulders, the long rangy body, the dusting of hair on strong forearms. Her eyes rested on his hands, long-fingered, broad across the palm, capable of such gentleness.

A huge lump seemed to catch in her throat. *I*

am painfully, idiotically in love with him, she admitted to herself for the first time. All of this self-reflection she'd been obliged to undergo had been for him. No, it was for Faith, too, and maybe herself, but it was *because* of Gray Van Dusen, part-time mayor, part-time architect. He had this way of looking at her as if she were the most beautiful, precious thing he'd ever seen.

She couldn't be imagining that. She couldn't.

Feeling a little as if she were suffocating, Charlotte took a deep breath.

"My leaving the way I did really didn't have anything to do with West Fork, although I did always hanker to find out what the big wide world was all about."

He nodded and took a swallow of his coffee.

Oh, just get it over with, she thought in misery. Hurrying, she said, "It was being an identical twin. I hated seeing Faith every day and knowing I wasn't distinct."

Gray went completely still. She didn't know how she could tell the difference, but there was one. An instant before, he'd been intent on her but otherwise relaxed. Suddenly he wasn't.

She bent her head and focused on the pale froth of iced coffee to avoid seeing his expression. "I loved Faith, of course. But my earliest memory is of looking at her and seeing myself. I felt this…I don't even know what to call it. Terror. As if I wasn't real. How could I be, if there was another me?" She ran a fingertip around the rim of the mug, struggling to calm herself. "I threw temper tantrums every time Mom tried to dress us in the same outfits, and I was rude to anyone who gushed about how cute we were, looking *exactly* alike."

In a strangely neutral voice, he asked, "You didn't feel any bond with her?"

"Of course I did!" Distress was making her own voice high, thin. "Especially when we were little, we were best friends. But all the time, I felt like someone with major claustrophobia being buried alive. I had this desperate need to rip my way free. Even when I managed to hide it, though, Faith always knew."

"That must have hurt her," he said, sounding hard.

"Yes." Charlotte realized she was rocking slightly, as if she were trying to comfort herself. She hoped Gray hadn't noticed. "It got worse and worse," she admitted. "Her being hurt, and me feeling guilty, which made me even more frantic to get away where no one knew I was a…a clone. I didn't want anyone to be able to read my mind the way she could. Or me to be able to read anyone else's. I wanted to be separate, alone, in the worst way."

"God." Gray slammed his mug down on the

railing, coffee sloshing. Stalking away, he didn't notice. He swung back, took an incredulous look at her and paced the other way.

He was furious, Charlotte was shocked to see. Not disappointed in her, not disgusted, but angry. *Why?* she wondered on one level, even as she scrambled to reassemble all the defenses he had spent the past weeks dismantling. This was going to be as bad as she'd feared. No, worse. Even as anguish swept over her, she told herself she had to pretend. She couldn't let him see how much it hurt that he wasn't even trying to understand what it had been like for her.

He stopped at last, right in front of her, forcing her to look way up to meet the storm in his eyes. "There's something I haven't told you about myself. I'm a twin, too." Muscles knotted in his jaw. "I *was* a twin. Until my brother died. We were ten years old."

"Oh, no," Charlotte whispered.

"We were riding our bikes. Racing down a hill in town. Gerrit was ahead. Just a few feet, but…" He stopped and scrubbed his hand over his face. "Neither of us noticed the car coming on the side street. Gerrit slammed right into it. I shot past the rear bumper. He suffered massive head trauma and went into a coma. He was dead two days later."

"Oh, Gray." Pain for him swelled inside her

until there was no room to breathe. "I'm so sorry. I suppose that's why your parents..."

"Yeah. They couldn't get over it. I guess the only way to move on was to start fresh without the other person to remind them."

"But...they still had you."

"Yeah, they did."

Merciful heavens. Had he grown up knowing that just *looking* at him hurt both his parents?

Yes, she thought in horror. He must have.

Gray was staring at her, his expression stony. "I've spent the rest of my life missing my brother and everything I lost that day. The same kind of bond that you couldn't stand and did your damndest to cut."

"Then you should be dating Faith instead of me!" Charlotte cried. "You'd be the perfect couple."

He swore, reached down to grab her arms and hauled her to her feet, where she collided against him. His mouth came down on hers with a ferocity that wasn't anything like him. He tasted of anger and frustration, his fingers were biting painfully into her flesh, but despite everything Charlotte opened her mouth and kissed him back.

A groan tore its way free from his chest. She felt the vibration of its passage. He quit kissing her long enough to mutter, "But it's you I want.

Goddamn it, it's you." The next second his mouth covered hers again, still hungry but more gentle this time. His tongue slid over hers, demanding but coaxing, too.

Charlotte's knees buckled and she flung her arms around his neck to hold on. Her whole body had gone soft. Melted, like the vanilla ice cream she'd watched his tongue slide over that day at Tastee's. Sweet and irresistible and unstoppable. She wanted Gray like she'd never wanted anything or anybody in her whole life.

Still kissing her, he lifted her into his arms and carried her inside. He strode across the living room, apparently not needing to look where he was going until he reached the top of the stairs. He took those slowly, licking and biting her throat and squeezing her breast in one large hand.

She was whimpering, which embarrassed her, but she seemed to have zero self-control right now. She'd tangled her fingers in his hair, which had a texture like the heaviest of raw silk, and her body curled around him as if she were trying to *meld* with him.

He didn't so much lay her on his bed as he did fall with her. Neither of them seemed to want to allow even an inch of space between themselves.

His mouth was more potent than any painkillers they'd given her at the hospital. He shoved his hand up under her camisole and massaged her breast, his palm rubbing her nipple until it was unbearably sensitive and she was arching off the bed and moaning.

Gray rolled so that she was on top and he could wrench her camisole off. He wrestled with the button and zipper holding her skirt on, and then that was gone, too, her panties with it. Once she was naked, his hands moved over her as if he were a blind man learning her shape, savoring what he found, wondering. Charlotte pressed her face to the juncture of his neck and shoulder and kissed him openmouthed, tasting him, licking the urgent beat of his pulse when she found it.

The sound that came from him finally was almost inhuman. He flipped her over again, rising just far enough to tear his shirt over his head and unzip his jeans. She caught a glimpse of blue boxers, and then even those were gone and all she saw was him.

Charlotte couldn't help herself. She laid her hands on his chest and explored it with all the wonder she'd imagined him feeling earlier. His muscles jerked as her fingertips slid over them. The texture of his chest hair was fine, silky. His stomach was rock hard.

As was his penis. She touched him tentatively, then more boldly when he knelt there on the bed looking down at her with hot, hungry eyes. When she stroked him, then squeezed, he groaned.

"Charlotte, are you on birth control?" His voice was so rough, she wouldn't have known it.

"No." Her eyes widened. They couldn't possibly have come this far and have to stop. "Oh, no! You don't have..."

"Yeah. I do. Just...damn it. Give me a minute." He left her long enough to open a drawer on his bedside stand. She heard the package rip, then watched as he sheathed himself. She wished he hadn't had to. She wanted him bare inside her, sleek and smooth.

It didn't matter. Charlotte wanted him any way she could have him. She held her arms wide and he came to her.

This kiss was desperate, deep and erotic. His tongue thrust and hers parried. The hand that wasn't wrapped in her hair stroked over her belly and slid lower, where she was already slick and so ready, so very ready, her hips bucked at the feel of his fingers.

He suckled her breasts, giving each a turn, the tug so strong she felt it down to her toes. And then he was parting her legs and pressing against her. She lifted her hips and he thrust, going so deep she had the dazed sense that he really was part of her now. Even though she *wanted* him to move, something like grief clutched at her when

Gray started to pull back. Charlotte wrapped her legs around him tight, determined to hold him.

He growled, "Damn it, Charlotte. Let me..."

For a moment it seemed they fought each other, but then he grasped her hips and lifted her. His body flexed and he went deep again, retreated and plunged, the strokes hard and fast. He was shoving her deep into the mattress.

Just before she convulsed, she opened her eyes and looked at his face. His usual mask of calmness had been ripped away. His skin was stretched tight over cheekbones sharper than she remembered them. His lips were pulled back from his teeth into something like a snarl. Sweat dampened his hair. His eyes were almost black, any semblance of control gone.

As was her own. She cried out as her body spasmed, the indescribable pleasure washing through her. Her release pulled him over with her. His whole body went rigid and he whispered "Charlotte" against her neck, as if her name was the only thing that anchored him.

She lay lax beneath him, even her arms falling loose. She had never in her life felt so utterly boneless, so incapable of moving. Gray was heavy, but she didn't want him to move, either.

At that moment, she knew what had been wrong with every other relationship she'd ever had. This, she thought, stunned, wasn't sex. It was something else entirely. It seemed as if every wall she'd ever built had cracked and fallen, leaving her completely vulnerable.

This was intimacy. She'd forgotten to protect herself. Any part of herself.

As her body cooled, as reason returned, Charlotte's fear returned to her stronger than it had ever been. What she'd just done with him defied every rule she'd lived her life by.

She wanted this. She wanted him.

But she'd been *born* with a primal fear of a connection that went so deep she couldn't deny it. What if she let herself love him, let him love her, and then that panic resurfaced? What if she couldn't live without her defenses?

She would hurt him terribly. And herself, perhaps past bearing.

I have to think about this. Great wings of fear were already beating in her chest. *I have to be sure.*

She couldn't think when she was with him. Not the way she had to. Thank God she had an excuse to leave West Fork, to use distance to regain perspective.

A thought niggled—she might be taking entirely too much for granted. Gray had never said a word about love. He'd been angry, earlier. He'd still wanted her, but now he had had her. Maybe now that he knew what ugliness she carried inside, this—what they'd just done—had been closure for him, not a beginning.

Maybe she was the only one who would be devastated.

SUNDAY MORNING ALWAYS STARTED SLOW. People in West Fork tended to be churchgoers. One early-bird browser had come and gone when Faith quit rearranging the display of jams, which had looked just fine before she began nudging and stacking and unstacking.

"Rory called last night."

Charlotte had just pulled the feather duster out from under the counter. The dust from the parking lot had a way of seeping in and laying a gray film over everything, given a chance. They had to whisk it away constantly, especially from the vintage glass and china.

Faith's tone was so matter-of-fact, it took the content of what she'd said a second to sink in.

Then Charlotte froze. "*What?*"

"While you were out last night." Her throat worked. "He said he's in Idaho now and that he won't be coming back."

"And you *believed* him?"

"He said losing me made him crazy, and he's sorry. He…he wanted to know how bad you were hurt. I think it really scared him, what he did to you."

"Why would that bother him any more than what he did to you?" Charlotte asked.

Her sister met her eyes so reluctantly, Charlotte knew Faith wanted to believe him. Wanted it with all her heart.

"Because it wasn't you who made him so angry. He's never attacked anyone before, you know. Only me."

Charlotte's eyes narrowed. "Are you so sure? Haven't you wondered about girlfriends before you?"

"You mean, I'm the only one who didn't have enough pride to ditch him at the first hint of violence?"

"No, I'm saying that he wants you to think it's his deep passion for you that makes him crazy. But I saw the look on his face when I ordered him off the property. I think he might have hit me if Gray hadn't walked in right then. You can't trust a word he says."

Faith sighed and her shoulders sagged. "I don't. I'm not that big a fool, Char. Never again."

"No." Charlotte dropped the feather duster on the counter and went around the end to hug her twin. "I can see how strong you are. You were ready to swing that baseball bat, and now you're carrying a handgun and you know how to use it." She shook her head. "What's the world coming to?"

Faith gave a laugh, if an abbreviated one. "Lord knows. Think about it. Here you are, back in West Fork living in your old bedroom, selling jams and hand-painted signs, and helping Daddy to the bathroom."

They both laughed then, shakily but with genuine humor. A final squeeze, and they stepped back.

"Did you call Ben?" Charlotte asked. "Tell him what Rory said?"

"No. I don't really know anything. Rory could be lying about where he is. Not to mention his intentions. And…I don't want to talk to Ben. Not for any reason."

After a moment, Charlotte nodded. She could understand that. She was feeling a little hostile toward Ben Wheeler herself right now.

"Faith," she said, then hesitated. "I have a couple of job interviews this week."

Faith's eyes widened, then darkened. "Oh."

"Tuesday, at a company in Redmond. And then Thursday down in the Bay Area."

"Oh," Faith said again.

"I'm going to leave Tuesday morning. I have to get to a salon." She tugged at her hair. "I'm hoping you have a suit I can borrow, by the way. Otherwise, I'll have to add shopping to the agenda. I have a Wednesday-morning flight, so I'm just going to spend Tuesday night at an airport hotel."

"And then? After the interviews?"

"I don't know," Charlotte admitted. "I think I'll put my condo on the market. Even if I stay in San Francisco, any job is likeliest to be in Silicon Valley, and I don't want that kind of commute."

"Daddy's doing really well," Faith said steadily. "We don't need you as badly anymore. What you did for me...for us..." She drew in a breath. "I can't ever thank you enough."

Charlotte made a rude sound. "He's my father, and you're my sister. I'll be back, Faith. Often. Maybe even to stay. I just...have to do some thinking."

"About Gray."

"Yes." She meant to smile, she really did, and make this breezy. She failed.

"You're in love with him."

"Stupidly."

"And he's in love with you?"

She closed her eyes. "I... Actually, I have no idea. I thought so, but..."

"But?"

She shrugged, although not carelessly enough. "He hasn't said. Turns out he had a twin brother, Faith. Gerrit. He died in an accident when they were ten. I'd just told Gray how I felt about being a twin, and he went off the deep end. We had sex, but he just drove me home afterward. He didn't say a word about love or even when, or if, I'd see him again." She had to press a hand to her chest, where it hurt so much. "It's probably a good time for me to take some time away. Lately I've been feeling like a cat that accidentally got shut in the dryer and thumped around a few times."

Faith flung her arms around Charlotte again. "But you will be back? Promise?"

"Promise." They hugged and held each other close. "I love you," Charlotte whispered, and her sister whispered back, "I love you, too. I always have, even when I was hurt and mad."

Charlotte sighed, finally. "I don't deserve you any more than that creep Rory did."

Faith's chuckle was a pleasant vibration. "Yes, you do. He doesn't."

Just then, two cars pulled in and parked just outside the barn doors. The sisters separated, smiled at each other with a softness that hadn't been there for a long time, wiped their damp eyes and turned to face the beginning of the Sunday afternoon onslaught.

DISMAYED THAT GRAY HADN'T CALLED or come by since dropping Charlotte off Saturday night, Faith prepared to drop off her sister Tuesday morning. He could have stopped Char from going, and she couldn't help wondering why he hadn't. She'd seen the way he looked at her sister, and would have sworn he was in love with her.

But what did she know? She wasn't exactly the most perceptive when it came to men!

The hour was early, the air still cool even as the sun climbed. No matter what else was happening in her life, Faith always loved the first day of school. She had when she was a student, and even more now that she was a teacher. She felt steady today, strong. A week ago, she would have been crumbling at the idea of Char going away again. But she was prepared now, in a way she hadn't been.

She couldn't carry the handgun with her at school, of course, but she intended to have it in the car, hidden in the glove compartment. It would be in her purse at home, which she would keep close by even when she was in the barn. And when she slept, she had made a habit of tucking it under the extra pillow on her bed. She could slip her hand under there in a second. If Rory ever really surprised her—and she was a heavy enough sleeper that he could—she might not have a chance to open the drawer on the bedside stand.

Faith hadn't told her sister about the last part of her conversation with Rory. It was just more of the same, she'd thought. Nothing that would help the police catch him, or her predict whether he was really done with her or not. She wanted to believe he just had to have the last word, that it was his way of holding onto his pride.

After sounding so repentant, he'd said, "If I'm back in West Fork visiting my parents, can I stop by and see you, Faith?"

"Please don't." She groped for a way to tell him they really were done, and found it. "I'm in love with someone else, Rory."

Which was the truth. She didn't have to tell her ex-husband that the man she'd fallen in love with didn't return her feelings.

There had been a long silence. She let herself hope Rory was accepting the finality of what she'd said.

But then—and this was the part that worried her—he said, "What about your wedding vows? Do you ever think about what you promised?"

Yes. That was why she'd forgiven him back then, and had continued to do so time and time again. But she'd finally run out of forgiveness. That last time, Rory had come too close to freeing her from those vows by killing her.

'Til death do us part.

"I don't like the idea of you with anyone else, Faith," he said, his voice sounding raw, and ended the call.

A threat? Or a last swelling of grief for what he'd lost? Faith couldn't begin to guess. All she knew was, if he came back, she'd be ready for him this time.

She and Char said their goodbyes in front of the car rental place in Marysville. It had seemed most logical for her to rent a car to get her to the salon, her job interview and then the airport.

They hugged one more time, and Faith drove away, on her way to school. There seemed to be a fissure in her chest, both painful and sweet. She could hardly tear her gaze from Char, diminishing in her rearview mirror. Going back to California. And yet, Faith was amazed to understand that distance didn't have anything to do with what they had recaptured.

She had her sister back, and nothing else in the world meant more than that.

CHAPTER FOURTEEN

EVEN BEFORE HE DROPPED off Charlotte at the farmhouse that night, Gray was already kicking himself for getting mad. His reaction to her story made no sense; she couldn't help how she felt, and she'd clearly suffered enough anguish without him dumping more guilt on her. And his loss had nothing to do with hers.

By morning, he realized was going to have some serious ground to make up to her. After they'd made love, she'd obviously wanted to go home. She had been quiet and withdrawn rather than prickly. Gray would a thousand times have preferred bristles. Charlotte shrinking inside herself worried him far more than her temper did.

On his way to the airport, he'd left a message on her cell-phone voice mail, begging her to call him.

By that night, she hadn't.

He wanted to believe she was ticked at him and determined to make him suffer, but he couldn't, not quite. He tried her again from his hotel in

Spokane, but this time she'd either turned the phone off or had let the battery run down.

He lay on the pillow-top hotel bed and stared at the ceiling, frustration tying his stomach in knots. Was he back to "go" with Charlotte? Would she make an excuse when he asked her to dinner again? Whip out the back door of the barn if she saw his car pull in at the front? Would her eyes snap with blue fire if he edged too close and made her want something she was apparently highly resistant to having?

The temptation to fly home in the morning was huge. But he was here now, and he should at least walk the site, show his sketches to the client and talk to the contractor to be sure his ideas were doable. The timing stunk, but his campaign to win Charlotte was ongoing anyway. A couple of days wouldn't make that much difference. And maybe she'd cool off, even miss him. She knew when he was coming home.

He'd have laughed, if he hadn't had that sick feeling in his stomach. He recognized it as considerably more than just frustration. Damn it, *he* missed *her.* He wanted to touch her, kiss her, have the hair at his nape stirred by the energy force field that she exuded.

Right now, he would have been content to hear her voice.

Moira had called twice on Monday and once on

Tuesday with various questions. Gray had taken phone calls from the West Fork public works department, from parks maintenance and from the city clerk's office.

But none from Charlotte.

He got in at SeaTac at eight-thirty Tuesday evening. His drive home took him by the Russell farm, but by then the lights in the house were out, and although his foot momentarily lifted from the gas pedal, he made himself continue on. At nearly eleven o'clock, it was too late to stop by. The moment he let himself in the front door at home, Gray went straight to his home phone and checked messages. There were a couple, including one from his mother, who didn't like to call his cell phone because she was sure she'd be "bothering him." None from Charlotte.

He carried his suitcase down to his bedroom and set it on a chair. He knew he should take a shower, but he couldn't seem to move. All he was doing was standing there, staring at the bed where he'd made love to Charlotte. Nothing in his life had prepared him for what he felt when he joined his body with hers. Technically, he'd been the one inside her, but she had filled an empty well in him. Despite friends, even a few semiserious relationships with women, he had been lonely most of his life until he met Charlotte. Why she, and only she, completed him, Gray had no idea, but that's what it felt like.

The idea of getting in that empty bed by himself was nearly unbearable.

A raw sound escaped his throat, and he turned and blundered for the bathroom. This was ridiculous. He'd see her in the morning. Impatient city officials could damn well wait for their mayor to put in an appearance. He needed to know how much damage he'd done to his courtship—and he couldn't think of a better word to call the delicate construction of a relationship with her. He would know when she saw him and her eyes betrayed what she felt.

He slept poorly and was up early. So early that waiting until anything approaching a respectable time just about killed him. At eight, he lost patience and drove to the farm, pulling in just as Faith was opening her car door, about to get in.

When she saw him, she waited until he parked and got out. Her expression seemed cool. "Gray."

Noticing that she wore slacks, a blouse and real shoes rather than summer flip-flops, he nodded. "You're back to school."

"That's right. Did you need something?"

"I came to talk to Charlotte."

Her gaze flicked over him, reminding him

uncomfortably of her sister's. "You might have wanted to do that a few days ago."

The nerves in his stomach congealed into a hard ball. "What do you mean?" he asked, hearing the roughness, the panic, in his voice.

"She's gone," Faith said.

"Gone?" Dazed and sick, he waited for the hammer stroke her confirmation would be.

Faith's expression changed. "Gray, you dropped her off Saturday night. That was three and a half days ago."

"She knew I was going to be out of town."

"She sounded like she hadn't heard from you. She said she didn't know when or if she'd see you again."

The burning in his gut could have been an ulcer. Charlotte had felt rejected. He'd done that to her. Not sure it was any excuse, he said, "I called Sunday morning. I left her a message asking her to return my call."

Faith studied him, frowning. "I…see."

"Where is she?" he asked desperately.

"Where were *you?*"

"I do out-of-town jobs sometimes. I'm designing a house for this guy in Spokane. It never occurred to me that Charlotte wouldn't still be here…." But that was a lie, he realized. Or an untruth, anyway. He *had* been afraid that she'd decide to run. That she would just disappear.

Apparently taking pity on him, Faith said, "She had a job interview yesterday, at a software firm in Redmond. She has another interview tomorrow, down in the Bay Area. San Mateo, or Palo Alto. I can't remember. She spent last night at an airport hotel, and she's flying to San Francisco this morning."

He felt flat-out fear. If Charlotte left now, went back to her condo and the emotionally barren life that she'd built to protect herself, she'd never come back. Not to him. To see her sister and her dad, sure. But Gray would have lost her.

Maybe his certainty wasn't rational, but there it was, a jagged chunk of rock in the morass of all his other emotions.

"When?" he asked hoarsely. "When is her flight?"

Faith's eyes widened. "Um…I don't have it written down. There wasn't any reason… Let me think. She grumbled a little, because she had a choice of crack of dawn and almost midday, and she went with the midday. Eleven-thirty, I think. Or eleven-forty. Something like that."

His muscles had tensed. "The airline?"

"Virgin America. She said they had the best rate…."

Faith hadn't even finished by the time a couple of long strides took him back to the driver side of his car.

"You're probably too late," Faith called after him. "By the time you get there, she'll have long since gone through security."

He looked at her over the roof of the car. "I have to try. If she calls..." His throat closed.

She nodded. "Good luck, Gray. Char needs to be loved."

He sucked in a painful breath and nodded. "I think she knows I love her. Why else would she pack up and leave the minute I turned my back? Without calling to let me know?"

Faith didn't say anything. She didn't have to. Gray could see in her eyes that she knew why her twin had fled with no advance warning.

Gray backed out and left so fast, he was a mile down the highway and could still see the cloud of dust floating above the Russell farm.

JUST THROUGH THE AIRPORT SECURITY check-point, Charlotte slipped her shoes back on, put her laptop back in its case and grabbed it and her carry-on. She glanced again at her boarding pass. Gate A14 would undoubtedly turn out to be in the far reaches of the airport terminal. She'd never yet taken a flight anywhere that left from a close-in gate. Charlotte had always suspected that the first gates were dummies, like the fake towns and houses she'd seen on the Universal Studio tour. Probably the people slumped in the waiting areas were extras. Who paid them she hadn't figured out, but otherwise it made sense, she thought.

A14, she discovered right away from a directory, *was* at the very far corner of this wing of the main terminal. She trudged down the broad hallway, passing a bookstore and a Starbucks and various restaurants, but not tempted by any of them even though she had plenty of time to kill. Her mood had been strange since she'd gotten up this morning.

Or even earlier, she acknowledged, finally reaching the waiting area and claiming a seat at the end of a row. Maybe even since she'd hugged Faith goodbye and headed south in the rental car.

Or, worse yet, since Gray had given her a last, hard kiss before she got out of his car Saturday night.

She had been such a coward, not telling him about the job interviews or that she had to go back to San Francisco. Not returning his phone call. Running away when she knew he was out of town.

She'd been so sure she needed distance and time to think, to decide if everything she imagined she was feeling was some kind of weird delusion, probably brought on by the experience of going home again—*really* going home, not just visiting in body while leaving her spirit behind, the way she'd always done before.

For the first time, Charlotte admitted to herself that she might not be here at all if Gray had canceled his trip and showed up at the farm Sunday or Monday to insist they talk.

Or even if he'd said more when he called. His brief message had been remarkably unrevealing. If he'd really wanted to talk to her, to see her, it wasn't in his nature to politely wait to hear from her.

Charlotte shivered, hating to feel so desperate and uncertain. Life had been easier when she could enjoy friends or a date or even sex without ever feeling *need*.

Yes, she thought, life was easier before she lost her job, came home and met Gray. But had she been happy? Had she had one single moment in the past ten years that compared to what she'd felt in his arms? Or even what she'd felt talking to Faith, regaining at least the beginning of the closeness she'd never had with anyone else?

Until Gray. I could have it with Gray, too. Only…more.

Unless he didn't want her anymore. Or had never wanted more than a casual relationship—an affair.

No, she knew better than that.

I love him.

Staring straight ahead, scarcely aware of other travelers filling the seats around her, Charlotte reminded herself how scary it had been to know she'd offered him everything.

Heart, body and soul.

That was fanciful, but it's what it felt like. As if she'd have no secrets from him, was handing him the power to hurt her with barely a glance or a word.

But...would he? She remembered the expression on his face that night after the cherry bomb exploded through the window, when he walked past Faith and Ben and the EMTs as if they weren't even there, as if she was the only person he saw. And when he pushed aside the curtain in the emergency room in search of her and his eyes found hers. Her heart squeezed as she thought about that night: the tenderness of his touch and his kiss, the slow, deep sound of his voice and always the way he looked at her.

Why had that scared her so much? Right this minute, she wanted more than she had wanted anything in her life to throw herself in his arms and just hold on.

Charlotte thought back to the smothering, completely irrational panic that had so damaged her bond with Faith, and understood it no more than she ever had. When she searched inside herself now, she couldn't find it anymore. Was there any chance it hadn't all been her fault, that Faith was right? Charlotte didn't have any memories from when they were really young. Like most people, she could call up no more than snapshots until nearly kindergarten age. Faith might have been especially insecure, especially clingy. Maybe she hadn't felt whole on her own, so in some way she was trying to consume Charlotte so they could be one.

Maybe.

Maybe not.

Charlotte guessed they'd never know, not completely, and it didn't seem to matter so much anymore. The miracle was, they could be friends now, sisters, without those old fears holding sway.

I know who I am, Charlotte thought, *and I'm okay with myself.* She was embarrassed to have something so simple feel like a revelation.

I can love someone, deeply, completely, without losing myself.

The certainty swelled in her, calming her. The emotion seeping through her felt strangely like one of Gray's slow, thoughtful looks, or the glide of his thumb over her lips, or the lazy, confident sound of his voice when he said things like, "Who got us out of the corn maze?" Or, "I'm staying. I'll sleep on the sofa."

Or even just her name.

He made her feel safe, wrapped in certainty, even when she was teetering on the edge of panic.

Charlotte knew suddenly that she didn't want to take a job in California. Not if there was any chance at all that Gray really wanted her, or even if there was still hope that he *might* want more than that one night.

And…no matter what happened with Gray, she'd be there for Faith. Rory wasn't gone for good, Charlotte didn't believe that for a second. He was still a threat.

She'd have to go back to San Francisco and put her condo on the market, Charlotte realized, arrange for a moving company to pack her stuff and transport it. But today, all she wanted was to go home, to West Fork.

The decision made, she took out her cell phone and was surprised to see that it wasn't on. When she tried to turn it on, she discovered the battery was dead. She'd been too frazzled to remember to charge it. *Way to go,* she thought. Yesterday's interview had gone really well. She liked the company and the people she'd met, found the work she would be doing intriguing, and—maybe best of all—she'd be able to do a good deal of it from home. What if they'd tried calling to offer her the job?

What if Gray had called?

There wasn't anything she could do about it now. She'd call the personnel office at SysPro this afternoon when she got home and tell them she had been offered another position.

There were surely pay phones here at the airport. She could call Gray now, instead of doing something impulsive and stupid like wasting the money she'd spent on the airline ticket. But she wanted to see him, not just hear his voice.

Impulsive wasn't always stupid, was it?

Charlotte went up to the desk and told the Virgin America representative that something had come up and she wouldn't need her seat after all. She handed him the boarding pass and walked away, pulling her small carry-on suitcase and carrying her laptop slung over her shoulder. The trek back felt shorter; her steps became quicker and quicker, until she was nearly running.

GRAY STOOD OUTSIDE THE SECURITY LINE, scanning it one last time without hope. At this time of day, it was short. He'd already stopped at the Virgin America counter, where he had been told that Charlotte Russell had checked in.

Of course she had. It was now—he glanced at his watch—10:36 a.m. Her flight would be boarding in half an hour, taking off in an hour.

He had tried calling several times on the drive down, and again when he reached the airport.

Her damn phone was off again. Or still off. She sure as hell didn't want to talk to him.

His heart was still pounding, as it had been since he peeled out of the farm. Adrenaline surged through him, signaled by some primitive need that had forced him to take life-saving action.

Finally turning away, making himself start back toward the front of the terminal and the escalator that would return him to the parking level, Gray thought bleakly, *I* was *trying to save my life.*

Not in a simplistic outrun-a-mastodon kind of way, of course, but the truth was that he couldn't imagine life without Charlotte. How that could be, when he'd known her such a short time and she had been fighting against falling in love that whole time, Gray didn't know. But it was true.

He wouldn't give up, just because she'd gotten away today. Damn it, sooner or later she'd have to answer her telephone. Or he'd clear his schedule for a few days and fly down to San Francisco after her.

Telling himself that didn't seem to help. Despair had him in its grip. Give Charlotte a few more days, and she'd harden her resolve. By the time he saw her again, her brittle, pugnacious persona would have regained control. He didn't know if he could overcome her resistance in just a few days, and that's all he'd have if she wouldn't come back to West Fork.

His gaze had been restlessly searching faces as he walked, even though there was no reason whatsoever to think he'd spot her now, outside security with her flight time so close. Out of the corner of his eye he saw people streaming out of the secured area of the airport, most pulling suitcases and talking on cellphones or holding hands with a reunited husband or child. People who'd just gotten off an airplane.

In their midst was a slender woman with pale blond hair cut boyishly short. She was walking fast, weaving in and out, rushing somewhere.

Gray stopped so suddenly, someone ran into him. He staggered but didn't even look to see who it was, didn't hear anything said to him. He was staring at the woman—Charlotte—hurrying toward him in an airy aqua-colored skirt he recognized. The white shirt over a camisole—he knew them, too, and the flip-flops. She'd repainted her toenails in one of those purple shades. Plum, he thought it might be called.

She was close, about to pass right in front of him. Galvanized into sudden motion, Gray all but lunged forward and grabbed her arm.

"Charlotte."

She wheeled in alarm that became something else when she saw him. "Gray?" she whispered.

"I thought you were gone." His voice was hoarse. "Your phone has been off."

"I..." She blinked. "Yes. It's dead and I hadn't noticed."

"Charlotte," he said, low and husky, just before he pulled her into his arms. With a cry, she let go of her suitcase and flung her arms around his neck.

They stood there in the middle of the concourse with people parting to go around them, locked together as if nothing would ever separate them again. His face was pressed against the top of her head, to the short, soft hair that was somewhere between the color of a dandelion bloom and the puffy seedhead that would follow. She felt so fragile to him, and yet so vital. Her scent was tart, citrusy, very much Charlotte, who would never want to smell sweet.

He realized her laptop was wedged between them, and that someone had knocked over her suitcase, which now sprawled flat on the floor in the midst of traffic. Reluctantly, Gray loosened his hold on her and asked, "Where were you going, Charlotte?"

She tilted her head back to look up at him. Color ran over her cheekbones, and her voice was definitely shy. "Home." She hesitated, took a deep breath, and finished, "To find you."

"Faith said you have an interview tomorrow."

"I'm going to call to tell them I'm not interested in the job."

Gray had to close his eyes for a moment, his relief so huge he didn't know if he could contain it. When he opened them again, he said roughly, "I love you, Charlotte Russell."

"Gray!" The laptop dropped to the floor with a clunk and she plastered herself against him again, all but burrowing as if she couldn't get as close as she wanted to. "Oh, Gray," she mumbled against his chest. "I was so afraid..."

He felt the tension of her knuckles on his back. From the tug at his shoulders, he could tell she had grabbed his shirt and was clutching it for all she was worth. He would have liked to get closer, too. He wished desperately that they were alone, preferably at his house, where he could have carried her downstairs again to his bed.

"Afraid?" he questioned.

"That you despised me."

On a clutch of guilt and pain, he pressed his cheek against her head again. "I'm sorry, Charlotte. So sorry. I never quit loving you, but I was angry. It wasn't fair." He sighed. "Maybe we should go to the car, instead of talking about this in the middle of the airport."

"In the middle of…?" She raised her head and looked around, her eyes widening. "Oh! My suitcase…"

Gray held her arms when she would have twisted away to rescue it. "Wait. First, will you say it? Do you love me? *Can* you love me?"

She went very still in his grip, slowly raising her gaze to meet his. "I already do. So much," she said in a small, scratchy voice, "it scared me to death."

"I don't want you to ever be scared of me."

She gave him a tremulous smile. "I'm…not as scared as I was. I got brave enough to *not* get on that airplane."

"So you did." Mouth curving, he kissed her. Only briefly, giving himself barely a moment to feel her lips quiver under his. Then he said, "You don't have a car, do you?"

Charlotte shook her head.

"Then let's go."

He picked up her suitcase while she rescued her laptop, and they walked to the escalator and across the skybridge to the parking garage. The whole way he kept one hand on her, right at the small of her back where he could feel every subtle shift and extension of her muscles.

When they got to his car, he tossed her suitcase and laptop into the trunk, then held the door for her as she got in. He went around and got in on his side, put the key in the ignition, then groaned and turned and reached for her.

"Kiss me," he whispered. "Please kiss me."

She made a funny, desperate little sound and dove into his arms, as far as the console and gearshift allowed. When his mouth met hers, it wasn't at all gentle. Her lips parted and they kissed deeply. He cradled her face in his hands while she ran hers over him as if to be sure he was truly there, that she remembered his contours.

He pulled back far enough to say, "I want you," even as he pressed open-mouth kisses to her throat, the curve where neck met shoulder, the hollow above her collarbone. "I don't know if I can wait two hours."

"Conveniently enough," Charlotte told him, "there are lots of hotels only a couple of minutes away."

Gray pulled back. "You're a genius." He gave a quick grin as he started the car. "I wonder if any of them have mirrors on the ceiling."

"Ugh."

"Yeah, not actually all that appealing, is it?"

"No."

All he wanted was to look into her eyes as he made love to her. To see them cloud with passion, to catch every flicker of emotion.

They didn't talk until he turned into the first decent-looking hotel he saw. "Wait here," he told her, and went in to register. Then he moved the car and ushered Charlotte inside.

The minute they were inside the hotel room, he spun around and trapped her between himself and the door. She flung her arms around his neck and rose on tiptoe to meet his kiss.

He took her mouth voraciously, with everything in him. He couldn't seem to find any patience in himself, any self-control. His hands lifted her skirt and grasped her buttocks beneath her skimpy panties. He ground his hips against her and kept kissing her as his head spun.

When he lifted his mouth from hers, all he could say was "Charlotte" in a thick voice that he'd never heard before. He lifted her and carried her into the dim room, laying her atop the king-size bed and bracing himself with a knee between her thighs.

He got her shirts off, but not the bra. Finding and releasing the back catch seemed beyond the capabilities of his suddenly clumsy fingers. He suckled her breasts anyway, wetting the satin cups. He shoved her skirt up and yanked her panties down. Thank God he had carried a condom in his pocket since the first time he met her, or he didn't think he'd have been able to stop. Gray didn't bother shedding his own clothes, only yanking down his zipper and pushing down his trousers far enough to free himself.

He cursed, getting the condom on with shaking hands. And then he pushed her thighs apart and thrust inside her. He felt her arms and legs wrap around him and saw her blue eyes go blind with a kind of shock as she arched and cried out.

She reached a climax with shocking speed. Gray plunged deep only a few more times before his body bucked and he groaned. He collapsed heavily onto her instead of rolling considerately to the side. It was several minutes before he could summon the resolve to make himself move. Even then, he held her tight.

It was going to be a very long time before he'd be comfortable taking his hands off her, never mind letting her out of his sight.

She only nestled closer and gripped his T-shirt, just as she had earlier.

"It's going to be embarrassing," she murmured, "when we check out and the desk clerk realizes we only wanted the room for an hour."

Gray laughed. "I'll just leave a tip and the key. They have my credit-card number. We don't have to face anyone."

She raised her head and peered at him. "Do you think you can make it home now?"

As sated as he felt, still his muscles tightened. "Only if you're really coming home. With me."

Charlotte didn't hesitate. "Dad and Faith won't know I'm not in San Francisco. Although

I suppose I should call Faith tonight—she must have told you when my flight was."

"Yeah. She wished me luck."

Charlotte was quiet for a minute. "Gray…are you still mad?"

"God, no! I just…reacted. You couldn't help what you felt. And I can see that you'd do anything for Faith."

Some indefinable tension left her body. "I wish you'd said, when you left that message."

"Would you have stayed if I had done that?" he asked.

"I'm not sure," she admitted. "I don't know." Pause. "Probably not. I was pretty shaken up. Mostly because…"

"Of what you felt when we made love."

"Yes," she whispered. "It was so much. Too much."

"No. Not too much." He rolled onto his side, so he was facing her, and reached over her to turn on the lamp. He wanted to see her face when he proposed. But first he smiled and ran his fingers through her hair. "Cute."

Charlotte wrinkled her nose. "It was this, or dye it again."

"Uh-huh." He stroked her cheek, touched his thumb to her mouth. "So which is it? New you, or old?"

Her smile was sassy. "Which do you think?"

"New," he said in a husky undertone. "Definitely new."

"That's what I think, too." She nipped his wandering thumb. "You know, we could keep the hotel room for two hours."

"Yeah." He was already aroused again. "We could. But first..."

Something in his tone made her eye him warily. "First?"

"We haven't known each other very long."

"No."

He cleared his throat. "Are you really staying?"

"I'm really staying. I had an interview yesterday. Did Faith tell you?"

Gray nodded.

"It's a great job. I really want it. But no matter what, I'll hold out for one up here."

He sucked in a breath. "Will you marry me, Charlotte? I never believed in love at first sight, but it happened to me when I walked into the barn that day. I want you forever."

Her face lit, her eyes sparkled. "Yes! Oh, Gray, I love you!" She scrambled atop him, making him wince a few times even as he gathered her in. "You didn't think I threw away the cost of an airline ticket just so we could tumble in bed for a couple of hours, did you?"

"That did give me hope," he told her, his hands

framing her face again just so he could look at her.

Happiness, he thought, with a peculiar shaft of pain and pleasure, made Charlotte Russell truly beautiful. He had every intention of ensuring she stayed beautiful for the rest of her life.

"I love you," he told her, and drew her down to him until their lips met.

* * * * *

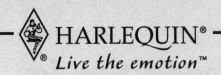

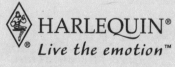

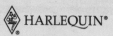

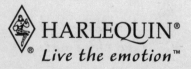

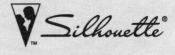